For our dead brilliant cousins,
Lizzie and Tom, Ben and Joe, Kate and Max

When I Told Will . . .

'Cool!'

I couldn't believe my ears.

'Perhaps you didn't hear me,' I said. 'I didn't say "I'm saving up for a skateboard" or "last night I saw a fox in my garden". I said "my dad is the Grim Reaper". Will, MY DAD IS DEATH!'

'That's so cool,' Will yelped, eyes like bagels.

'You don't think better words might be *weird* or *creepy*?'

'Coooool!' he said one more time, slowly. His mouth hung open like a broken snapdragon.

So, I had just dropped a bombshell – front-page news, the full enchilada, the biggest, maddest, most eye-stretching piece of information a boy could ever imagine: I live with Death. DEATH is MY DAD! And what did Will think?

He thought it was *cool*.

'What, Will? What's cool, *exactly*?' I was exasperated.

'What's out there and stuff, Jim. You know . . . How it's all connected.'

The whole world is connected is one of Will's sayings, and I tell you, he can find a link between anything – a Siberian hamster and a French baguette, a nose hair and a grain of rice. But my dad being Death and that being cool? Will's very own connection with reality was looking a bit shaky.

I snapped. 'Forget what's "out there". I'm talking about what's right here. Aren't you freaked out?'

The answer was no – Will wasn't the tiniest bit freaked out. 'So when does he go out and make people dead, then? Does he stalk the streets?'

'Of course not! He turns up when people are ready to die.'

'People call him? There's a hotline number?'

'No. He just pops round to their house and, er, makes them dead.'

'Urgh, that is horrid!' Will exclaimed, but there was a grin fixed from one ear to the other. I think he had Morbid Curiosity. It's when you're fascinated by death. I should know.

'So how does he actually do it? Is it like –' Will clutched his throat, pretending to strangle himself. 'Or how about –' He mimed stabbing himself in the heart.

I wondered if insanity was a side effect of morbid curiosity, because Will wasn't being very Will all of a sudden. My friend Will thinks *SpongeBob SquarePants* is an emotional roller-coaster, and he's not the type that likes blood, guts and violence. At a Romans dress-up day at school, we all came as centurions, naturally. Will came as a market fruit-seller.

Will put the imaginary knife into his heart and pulled it out again, laughing.

'Cool,' he said again, clutching his sides.

What I hadn't told him yet was that my dad, Death, was out to get Will's granny. Not cool. Not cool at all.

Chapter 1

But let's go back a bit. Back to when the world as I knew it changed forever. Back to when I found out that my dad was not Terry Wimple, Senior Accountant at Mallet & Mullet, but the Grim Reaper.

How did I find out? Let's just say that there were things about Dad being an accountant that didn't add up – including the fact that he's rubbish at maths. So if he wasn't an accountant, what was he? My investigations led me to his office, and what I saw there I'll never forget, unless Dad wipes my memory (I'll explain later). The Mallet & Mullet building was modern and shiny on the outside, but behind secret sliding doors there were fusty old corridors and ancient paintings and strange rooms – Brain Training rooms, Glove rooms, goodness-knows-what rooms and the General Office room. Things got super weird when I went in *there*. Offices normally have computers and printers and stuff, don't they? Well, there wasn't a computer to be seen. Not even a calculator. It was full of creaking machines and people dressed in black cloaks, who, when given a quick maths test, convinced me they weren't accountants either. None of them were. To cut a long story short, I confronted Dad with a theory. An impossible theory. He was Death. Only he went and admitted it!

So, there it is: Mallet & Mallet is a pretend accountancy company – a cover for The Dead End Office, where Deaths do their paperwork. And Dad and his team of Deaths are responsible for Natural Deaths in Greater London. They takes the oldies, basically.

When I discovered that, it should have been the end of the story. But it wasn't.

Usually my investigations, such as *My Roof: A Landing Pad for Aliens?*, have solid conclusions, like *No, the Patches on the Roof are Caused by Poor Insulation*. And then there's nothing much more to say (unless you want to talk about insulation. I don't). But this investigation was different. Knowing Dad's real job didn't provide me with a satisfying conclusion – it just made me want to know more. I had millions of questions, like *What is the Meaning of Death?* It made me want to jump in the deep end. Let me explain.

Some questions have a shallow end and a deep end, a bit like a swimming pool. You can touch the bottom easily with a simple answer, but if you're looking for a more complex answer you can quickly get out of your depth. It's one of Will's theories. He introduced it to me when I asked if he preferred roasted or salted peanuts. Will explained that the shallow-end answer was 'salted', but for a deep-end answer he'd need to ask more questions, like 'In what situation – extreme hunger or light snacking?' and 'Are there any other nut types on offer?' as well as 'How old are the nuts?' My best friend might act like he has marshmallow brains, but there are solid nuggets of biscuity brilliance inside Will Maggot's head. He's kind of shallow and deep, himself. Like a Wagon Wheel or a Tunnock's Teacake.

What does that have to do with *the Meaning of Death*? If you've done life cycles in your science lessons you'll know that death means there is no heartbeat or brain function. But that's just the shallow answer. Oh yes . . . Like Will's peanuts, the deep end of *What is the Meaning of Death?* is more complicated – it's a question made up of more questions, which I'll tell you in a minute. And I wanted the answers to those questions more than I wanted a lifetime supply of prawn cocktail crisps (which was quite a lot).

Of course, I asked Dad right away. After all, he was pretty much the expert on Death, and asking questions is what a healthy inquisitive kid is supposed to do. I said: 'Tell me more about death.' He said: 'I couldn't possibly burden you with the details, son,' and I said, 'Go on,' and he said, 'You should be living for the moment, not worrying about the end.' But I was worrying about the end – dying to know, in fact – so I fired the full list of deep-enders at him in one go:

What is the *meaning* of death?

How do you dead people?

Why do you dead people?

Do you *have* to dead people?

What happens if you *like* who
you're about to dead?

What would happen if you
refused to dead someone –

Actually, I didn't make it through the full list, because Dad stopped me. Not with one of our usual wordy jokes, like 'You're *dead* curious today, Jim' or 'You're making a *grave* mistake by asking me all these questions.' No. He stopped me with The Cold Eye.

My dad has a friendly face, like an old-fashioned policeman or a carol singer on a Christmas card. *So* friendly, you'd never expect it could look menacing or dangerous. But when Dad sucks in his cheeks and narrows his eyes, he can look surprisingly evil – like a vampire sucking a lemon. That, my friend, is The Cold Eye. Without saying a single word, The Cold Eye shouts, 'BACK OFF OR THERE'LL BE TROUBLE!'

The Cold Eye can't be ignored, so I did back off, quickly.

But the questions rattled around inside my brain, distracting me during the day and keeping me up at night. They were begging to be answered. And if Dad wouldn't give me the answers, I'd just have to go hunting for them. I picked a brand new project book off my shelf, unwrapped it, opened it, and wrote the title in bold letters:

What is the Meaning of Death?

I quite often use project books for my investigations. That's because if you write down everything you know (even stuff that seems irrelevant) you can sometimes fit it all together like a jigsaw and find the truth. It's what detectives do. *Nothing is strange when the truth is in range* – that's another one of Will's sayings, and it's one that makes a lot of sense (a lot of his really don't, at least not to me).

Let me show you what I wrote.

WHAT IS THE
MEANING OF DEATH?

Things I know about
The Dead End Office

Fact 1. Dad is in charge of Natural Deaths

Dad only does Natural Deaths. He takes away old people whose time is up.

Note: I don't know how he does it, but Dad says this is painless and I believe him, because he's a big softy.

Fact 2. The Misadventures Team

The Misadventures Team work at the scene of fatal accidents (unnatural deaths) to bring death quickly, so people don't suffer too much. They also take people who get really ill to stop their pain. And they help deal with Trouble Clients.

Note: Dad turned down a promotion to Misadventures because he's scared of blood.

Fact 3. Trouble Clients
Trouble Clients are people who Dad is having trouble getting rid of, and Dad's boss gets cross if there are too many of them.

Note: I think some medicines get in the way of the death process.

Question: Why are Trouble Clients a problem for The Dead End Office? (NB, see title of this investigation.)

Fact 4. Deaths wear Nifty Trainers
These trainers are designed for speed and silence, so Deaths can work quickly, undetected.
Note: They look quite comfortable, although I haven't tried any on yet.

Fact 5: Memory Wiping
Dad did special Brain Training and can wipe people's memories.
Note: I do not want this to happen to me – ever.

Conclusion: I do not have enough facts to form an opinion about the Meaning of Death.

Note: I need more facts.

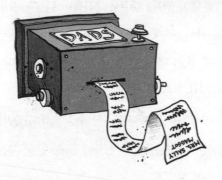

Chapter 2

There were facts and answers in Dad's study.

There had to be. It was the one room in our house that was off-limits, and when Dad went in there he closed the door firmly behind him so we couldn't see in. When he went out of the house he locked it, but I knew he kept the key in the bottom of the umbrella stand. I was itching to get inside and nose around, and any kid with a teaspoon of naughtiness would; but I just couldn't do it – I'd made a promise to Dad, and trust is a big thing between us. It's our code, our bond, our father–son special handshake. There was no way I could break it.

So, I was just going to have to collect my facts another way. Dad's office was out of bounds. For good.

Well, out of bounds until a week later, when Hetty lunged at me with a pair of scissors, and everything changed.

Hetty is my six-year-old sister. She's as cute as pie. Everyone says 'awww' when they see her. But Hetty is devious. She steals money (to save up for a horse), and all her games involve physical pain. Or a punishment, at least. Now you know that, you're thinking, *There's no way she's cute as pie!*, but actually, she is. She's my little sister and I'd do anything for her. Well, almost anything. I wouldn't let her cut my hair.

Not in a million years. She cuts her own and I've seen the results . . .

So when, in the middle of watching *Doctor Who*, she randomly declared herself to be 'Hetty Hairdresser – the Gold Standard Stylist' and went to fetch the kitchen scissors, I needed a hiding place, and fast. It had to be somewhere good. Somewhere she wouldn't dare go.

The study! She wouldn't dare go in the study. Neither would I. Or *would* I?

From what I've seen in films and on the news, when there are 'exceptional circumstances' rules that are made for everyday life go out the window. Windows themselves, for example. On a normal day you'd never climb out of the window, but if there's a fire, then climbing out of the window would be totally acceptable. Even encouraged! I applied this thinking to

Dad's study: on a normal day no one is allowed in Dad's study, but on a day when Hetty is determined to cut your hair into an embarrassing wonky bowl shape? Then, yes, going into Dad's study would be totally okay. Seeing as Dad nearly lost an earlobe to Hetty Hairdresser, he'd have to agree if he found out.

But he wouldn't find out – he had just started watching his favourite *Mr Bean* episode and would be glued to the sofa for at least twenty minutes . . .

With butterflies in my tummy, I pushed the door open and stepped inside Dad's study, letting the door close quietly behind me. Maybe I was just nervous, but the room had a strange air – still and quiet, as if time had frozen. I ran my fingers across the bookcase. It was full of big, heavy, leather-bound books with titles like *Laws for Misadventures*, *Troubleshooting the*

Deceased, *Death Dictionary* and *Natural Death Protocols*. There were piles of papers and boxes stacked in the middle of the carpet – shoe boxes, glove boxes, box files. But I found myself drawn to the desk in the bay window – a large oak table with deep drawers and a green leather top, like something you'd find in the office of a General or a Prime Minister. On the desktop were feather quills, pots of ink, an ancient telephone made of metal and wood, just like the ones I'd seen at The Dead End Office – and spread open was a large diary. It was full of notes:

Full office meeting with Pop-Ins – Boardroom 3 p.m.
Discuss calibrating HEX to accommodate eyebrow data
Don't forget: regional death file swap

Eyebrow data? Pop-Ins? Regional death files?

> *Misadventures visit cancelled – on*
> *stand-by for earthquake in Yorkshire*
> *Bristol wants to borrow some Deaths.*
> *Send five on Wednesday.*

Earthquake in Yorkshire? Borrow Deaths?

> *Deal with Trouble Clients*

I knew what Trouble Clients were – kind of; they were the people who dodged death – but how was Dad going to deal with them? How was he going to kill them? How would he feel when he was causing their deaths? The deep-end questions began pouring in, thick and fast, but they were interrupted by the sound of footsteps outside the door.

'Snip, snip, Jimble Wimble,' came Hetty's threat, muffled by the door. 'You're not in there, are you?'

If Hetty knew I was in Dad's study I'd be in big trouble. My little sister is masterful with secrets – and blackmail. She uses information like ninjas use nunchuks. I darted into a corner behind the bookshelf, just in case she peeked through the keyhole.

I held my breath and waited for her to go (which would probably take a while, Hetty could be quite persistent). I didn't waste my time, though. I cast my eye around the room, looking for details and facts for my investigation into *The Meaning of Death*. I noticed a white glove in a glass case, a black cloak on a hook behind the door, a pair of nifty trainers I briefly considered trying on – and then a noise, a tiny rasp no louder than a mouse sneeze, drew my eye across the room.

There, mounted on the wall, was a plain wooden box with a roll of paper jutting from its mouth like a tongue. The box rasped and the tongue jerked forward once, then twice, like a lazy till receipt. I heard Hetty's footsteps climbing the stairs, and her threat of 'Snip Snip' fade into the distance. The coast was clear. I jumped up to take a closer look at the box. A small brass plate on top of the box said *DADS*, but apart from that there was no more clue to what it was or what it did – just the tickertape paper, which was growing longer. I held it in my hands. There was something printed on it – a list of names! Another rasp and the paper spat forward, with a new name at the top. What was this? Names of Deaths who Dad worked with? Trouble Clients perhaps, like the ones I'd seen pinned on Dad's wall at The Dead End Office? The paper jolted and I ran my eyes to the top of the tickertape. Another new name.

I gasped, because this time it was a name I knew. *Mrs Sally Maggot.*

What was she doing there?

It was like seeing your head teacher in a tracksuit buying baked beans at the supermarket – you know who it is, but it feels all wrong. Seeing the name of my best friend's gran coming out of Dad's *DADS* felt very wrong indeed. I didn't understand. What was the box up to? And *DADS* didn't make sense. The letters must stand for something. If I could find out, then I might discover what all this was about . . . I looked around the room for clues. Then up at the bookshelf. *Bingo!*

Balancing on Dad's chair, I brought down

the *Death Dictionary*, nearly toppling under its weight, and laid it on the ground. It was covered in deep powdery dust; the thick pages were crinkled and brown and stiff. They were filled with inky handwritten sentences and sketches – diagrams of nifty trainers, stitched gloves, strange apparatus . . . I turned to the section marked D and found what I was looking for.

DADS

The Direct Action Death System is a messenger machine. Clients' death dates are calculated by the HEX machine. Workers input names of Clients scheduled to die into the central DADS machine and send them to Deaths for immediate action. The DADS itself contains no calculation machinery. See **HEX**.

I flicked to H. H for HEX. There was a complicated diagram of the HEX and I recognised it immediately as the giant machine I'd seen at The Dead End Office! A beast of a machine with rows of buttons, levers and a display with numbers that spun like symbols on a fruit machine. Workers had been scribbling the numbers down eagerly and I was about to find out why.

The HEX (Human Existence machine)
The HEX uses personal data, gathered and supplied by the Population Institute (abbrev. Pop-In), to calculate a person's death date. See **DADS**. *See also* **Client**. *See also* **Population Institute**.

So that's what the Pop-Ins were. But Clients, scheduled for death?

Client

Client is the term given to a person who is scheduled to die. A Client's death date has been calculated by the HEX machine. On a Client's death date, his or her name is distributed through DADS machines for immediate action. See **HEX.** *See also* **DADS.** *See also* **Trouble Client.**

I rested back on my heels and processed what I'd just read.

a) The big HEX machine calculates death dates

b) Clients are people whose death date has come up

c) Client names are sent to Deaths through the *DADS,* for immediate action

I tried to work it all out in my head. Why did it have to be immediate? Were they baddies, evil-doers, threats to the universe? Granny Maggot – threat to the universe? Hardly . . . No! Suddenly I understood. Immediate meant right away, here, today, now.

The truth hit me like wagon wheel (a real one, not the marshmallowy kind): it was Sally Maggot's day to die. Sally Maggot – my best friend's gran – was going to get deaded.

By my dad. Before the day was done.

Chapter 3

My dad is an orphan and Mum's mum lives on the other side of the world – so I can't pretend to be a granny expert. But I'm pretty sure the standard gran is supposed to give you money and sweets and say nice things. Mrs Maggot wasn't a standard gran.

Money and sweets? No chance, and as for saying nice things? Granny Maggot mostly said 'MYERGH' (like *ergh*, but from the back of the throat and more mucus-y). She said it for *yes*, *no* and *maybe*. It also had a meaning all of its own. I'd been to see her with Will a few times, and their conversations followed a pattern.

'Would you like me to plump up your cushions, Gran?'

'*Myergh.*'

'Shall I tell you about my day at school, Gran?'

'*Myergh.*'

'What have you been doing today, Gran?'

'*Myergh!!!*'

And if *Myergh* wasn't bad enough, she was just so . . . *depressing*! She was always saying things like: 'I can't bear this life – someone push me off a cliff!' and 'Pop me in the oven and cook me at two hundred degrees' and 'Chop me up and feed me to the pigs, would you?'

One day she said: 'I wish I would die and be done with it – no one would miss me.'

At this, Will threw himself onto his knees like a rock guitarist and wailed: 'I'd miss you, Granny! I'd miss you so, so much. Don't cook yourself at two hundred degrees. Don't fall off a cliff. If you do, then I'm coming, too!'

That was when I realised how much Will loved her. He loved her to death. And I love Will. Not in a kissy kind of way – he's my best friend, and I hate seeing him hurt. Will hurts easily and very deeply. For example, it took him hours to stop shaking when the school bully, Jeremy Flowers, crushed a snail in front of him; and when his sister said she'd sacrifice him to the Devil for a new skateboard, he climbed inside his duvet cover and stayed there for two days.

Will just can't cope with nastiness on any

level, so I've always sworn to protect him. It's my job as his best friend. It's especially important because I think I'm his *only* friend, apart from Max. But Maximus is a giant African land snail and probably doesn't count.

Now you see why I found myself in a particularly awkward situation:

1) Will loved his gran – to death
2) My own dad was going to kill her – to death

But,

3) If I told Will what Dad was going to do, I'd be breaking my promise to Dad
4) If I let Dad kill Mrs Maggot, I'd be breaking my promise to protect Will

There was only one solution: I had to take Mrs Maggot off the death list. All I had to do was rip her name off, throw it away and the whole nightmare would be over.

I snatched the scroll of paper from the *DADS* machine.

But it wouldn't tear, no matter how hard I twisted it. I knelt down and grabbed the paper between my teeth and tugged and tugged. Nothing. It was some kind of super-tough tooth-resistant paper. I needed something sharp. I tiptoed out of the study and into the kitchen to find Mum's best scissors. Hetty had them, of course. And she was waiting for me.

'I knew you'd give in eventually,' Hetty sang, when I walked into the kitchen. She chop-chopped the scissors, menacingly. 'Pop yourself down on the chair.'

'Not now, Hetty.'

'Snip snip!'

'Give me the scissors, Hetty.'

'Only Gold Standard hairdressers are allowed to touch the scissors. You are a poo-standard hairdresser.'

'Give them to me, Heather,' I said. I use her real name when I'm trying to be serious.

'Poo-standard hairdressers are not allowed to talk to Gold Standard hairdressers in that tone of voice. As your punishment I will –'

'I'm serious,' I growled.

Usually, it doesn't matter what I say – Hetty does what she likes. But this time, she put the scissors on the table and stepped back. There was a smile in her eyes.

'I am giving you the scissors. And you are taking them from me. Do you agree?'

'Yes, Hetty. Thank you.'

'Don't thank me in words,' she said mysteriously, and walked out of the kitchen.

When Hetty is being mysterious, you should

be very worried. But I didn't have time to think about that. I had paper to cut, grannies to save, best friends to keep safe from emotional trauma. Promises to keep . . .

I went back to the study and attacked the paper with the scissors, until my fingers nearly blistered. But the scissors didn't make a mark on the tickertape, not even a nick in it. Dad must have a special implement – a supreme slicing blade or laser beam – but I could hear the closing theme to *Mr Bean* drifting from the living room, followed by the satisfied yawning sound Dad makes when he's having a stretch. Time was up.

I snuck out of the study, ran to my bedroom and shut the door. Before I forgot it all, I wrote down everything I'd discovered into my project book – the stuff from Dad's diary about earthquakes, Pop-Ins, death file swaps, Death borrows; and I wrote down everything I knew about the Human Existence and *DADS* machines as well as the tickertape of death. As I finished writing, I realised I was grinding my teeth. It must have been the tension – tension caused by being pulled in opposite directions, like a stretched elastic band. Did I protect Will, or Dad?

There was nothing for it. If I couldn't remove Sally Maggot's name from the list, then I'd have to remove the real Sally Maggot – in person.

It was time to make like a race car and put on my Formula Onesie.*

---

* It's a little saying I made up. Hope you like it.

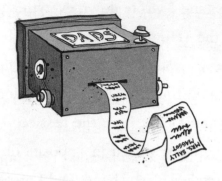

Chapter 4

I didn't get even get a toe into my (metaphorical) Formula Onesie when Mum and Dad cornered me.

'Come into the kitchen, Jim,' Dad said.

Had he found out about me being in the study? I quickly ran through my 'exceptional circumstances' speech in my head.

'Your mum is making something wonderful,' he added. I was relieved. 'Something wonderful'

was code for 'something absolutely disgusting'.
Dad needed my help.

If you haven't met my mum before, I'd better explain so you don't think I'm being rude about her cooking. Mum's a health nut. She owns an online health food shop called The Happy Husk and her hobby is creating recipes from the foods she sells – weird cakes and pies, but mainly smoothie drinks made out of nuts, seeds, stuff from the bottom of lawn mowers (it looks like) and dried-up berries that smell of wet dog. If you're around when Mum is making smoothies you're in trouble, because she's always looking for guinea pigs to try them out on.

'This is wheatgrass with lemon juice and some magic health powder!' Mum said, beckoning me to the kitchen table, where there was a huge jug of green liquid that looked like pond scum.

I sat down opposite Dad, who was looking distinctly nervous. Mum poured some of the liquid swamp into a glass and it slopped up the sides, leaving a gritty green trail. She held up the glass to the light triumphantly.

'Cheers! Natural goodness going down!'

She downed it in one, slammed the glass on the table top and held onto the kitchen counter to steady herself.

'Looks like natural goodness might come back up,' Dad whispered to me out of the side of his mouth.

'You alright, Mum?' I asked, trying not to laugh.

'No one said self-preservation was easy,' she muttered. I noticed a bit of green gunk caught in the corner of her mouth. 'Now, who's next?'

'What is the magic powder?' I asked, avoiding her question.

'New product. Japanese algae,' she spluttered. Some of the algae was stuck halfway down.

'So, it's *literally* pond scum!' I blurted, and I heard Dad cover up a laugh with a cough.

'Scum is not a very nice word, Jim. Try *spirulina* – you won't find a substance more packed with nutrients, you know. Says here on the packet that it can contribute to a longer, healthier life.'

I nodded to show I understood. But I didn't really. I mean, could an algae drink really extend your life? I looked at Dad, but his face gave nothing away. He just smiled affectionately at Mum. She held a glass out to him and nodded encouragingly. I saw a flash of panic on his face, but there was no escape. He held the glass to his lips for a moment – his eyes watered, his lips quivered . . .

'What are you calling this one, darling?' he

said, quickly putting it back down on the table, turning the glass round, pretending to admire its colouring. Mum always gives her concoctions cheerful names like Spring Clean or Happy Slurpie or Summer Daze.

'How about Poo Poo Wee Wee Juice?' said Hetty, breezing into the kitchen on her pink scooter, dragging Bo-Bo behind on a string. Bo-Bo is a teddy bear that looks like road kill.

'You don't have your helmet on, Hetty!' Mum gasped. Mum's concern for head safety is off the scale. I wore a homemade hat of bubble wrap for the first two years of my life.

'Hi, Dad,' chirped Hetty. 'Do you want to take me to the park?'

'Actually, Hetty, my strange-flavoured jellybean, all my colleagues are on holiday, so I'm on call. I'm afraid that means I need to do some work –'

Hetty wailed dramatically – only because she's a drama queen, not because she knows about Dad doing deaths. Because she doesn't. I mean, can you imagine what she'd do with that kind of information? She'd leave ninjas and their nunchucks for dust.

'I know, I know,' Dad soothed. 'I would have loved to go the park. So I'm sad, too.' Dad pulled a sad face and then pretended to cry, which made Hetty giggle. I saw him flick his eyes towards the cupboard at the back of the kitchen. Hetty's face lit up with a naughty grin. She crept behind Mum's back to where Dad kept a secret stash of chocolate biscuits.

'Take a couple for yourself, champ,' he whispered to me as he stood up from the table. 'Right, I'll be in my study. Doing paperwork. Knock if you need me.'

'I do paperwork too,' said Hetty, pulling a

piece of paper from her pocket. 'Here's a contract I made for you, Jim.' I took it from her suspiciously and put it straight in my pocket to read later. Hetty's contracts were never good news. 'You must honour it *today*, Jim. It's a today contract.' Clutching Bo-Bo in one hand and a fist of melting chocolate biscuits in the other, she skipped out of the kitchen.

My heart skipped, too, in panic. Dad was going into his office and I knew it wouldn't be long before he was out of the door with his list of Clients . . . I had to get going! There wasn't even time for chocolate biscuits. I needed a head start.

'Drink?' said Mum, hopefully.

After narrowly dodging a dose of Pond Scum, I called Will and we agreed to meet at the corner of my road *immediately*. I ran upstairs and packed a rucksack – project book, pencil, money, binoculars, put on my new baseball cap and raced out the door without telling anyone. Precious minutes would be lost if Hetty or Mum started up another conversation, and I was pumped, I was ready. I was ready to save Granny Maggot. I even had a plan.

The plan: if it was Granny Maggot's death date today – and I was pretty sure it was – then all I had to do was keep Mrs Maggot alive until tomorrow. That was twenty-four hours; in fact, it wasn't even that long, because some hours had gone already. By my calculations it was approximately fourteen hours. Easy peasy. All I had to do was keep her away from Dad, keep Dad away from me, and keep the secret to myself. In other words: kidnap a granny, run from death and not tell anyone. Okay, so it wasn't going to be all that easy. But I like to think I'm not the kind of kid that gives up when the going gets tough. Although I really, *really* had to get going.

Will didn't come and meet me immediately, like he said. He turned up fifteen minutes later. Fifteen whole minutes of Granny Maggot's life!

'Where on earth have you been, Will? You said you'd come quickly.'

'Everyone has a different pace, Jim,' he replied. 'Top speed of a snake is twelve miles

per hour. Top speed for an adult snail – one millimetre per second. See?'

'And what's your top speed, Will?' I quizzed crossly.

Will was completely unfazed. 'I can probably walk two and a half miles per hour. But if I'm reading at the same time, I slow down considerably.' Will held up his *Snail Enthusiast Monthly* magazine as an explanation. 'It just arrived in the post.'

This is typical Will. And I don't mean the marshmallow brains that yield biscuity brilliance, I mean his obsession with snails. He talks, sleeps and breathes snails (he doesn't eat them) and his favourite bedtime read is *The Big Book of Molluscs*.

'Okay, Will,' I said, trying to keep my calm. 'But can we walk and not read now?'

'Sure. What are we doing?'

'Well, today I thought we could visit your gran. Granny Maggot.'

'But I saw her yesterday.'

'And I think you should see her again today. Look, I want to start a new project and I need your help.'

'Always happy to help with a project, Jim. We could do "What happens when slugs meet snails", or how about this – "If you cut an apple into the shape of an orange and colour it orange, will it still taste like apple, or an orange?" Either way, I don't think my gran will be much help . . .'

'I've already decided on my project, actually,' I said, 'and it definitely involves your granny. I want to investigate whether –' (Help! I hadn't thought of this bit) – 'er, Random Acts of, er . . . Randomness, improve, er, um, life. For old people.'

'It wouldn't be that random, though, would it, because she's my gran, and we're related,' said Will.

'But she isn't *my* gran,' I said, thinking quickly. '*I'm* not related to either of you.'

Will nodded and twitched his nose. I could tell he was warming up to the idea. 'So why do you think randomness will improve her life?'

'Well,' I said, pausing to tie my shoelace, thinking of a reply. 'Old people do the same thing day after day. They have a routine. Perhaps if they did other stuff they hadn't planned to do, it would make them happier.'

'So what are we going to do with her?'

'We're going take her out for a day trip,' I said, smiling.

Will paused. 'She's not expecting us, though.'

'It's Unexpected Random Acts of Randomness, then.'

'But if something's unexpected it can give people a shock.' Will boggled his eyes at me like I had baked beans for brains. 'Shocks can kill old people, you know!'

Try your best mate's dad, I thought. But I couldn't say that to Will. He'd go into shock.

'We could give her sugar,' I suggested. 'Sugar helps stabilise people in shock. It's the only time sugar should be allowed, Mum says.'

'So when you went into shock after the hundred metres sprint on sports day . . .?'

'Yep,' I grinned. 'Faked it for a KitKat.'

Will rolled his eyes and laughed like a donkey.

'That's settled then,' I nodded. 'We'll take Granny Maggot sugar and she'll be fine.'

Will and I looked at each other and smiled.

'Battenberg cake!' we said at exactly the same time. And it wouldn't be for the first time . . .

Chapter 5

Granny Maggot lived in a retirement village, which is like a block of flats but horizontal because old people's legs aren't great at stairs. Granny Maggot was so bad at stairs she sometimes tripped over her own doormat and lay on her back like a big old beetle, legs kicking in the air. It's hard not to see the funny side. But right now I wouldn't have seen the funny side if a clown hit me with funny-side pie. And neither could Will – he was concerned that our failure to find Battenberg cake might result in shock and death.

'*Myergh*. It's you again,' said Mrs Maggot. 'What you doin' here?' She was wearing a brown badly fitting cardigan, fluffy slippers and a weird woollen dress with flowers on.

'We wanted to bring you some Battenberg cake,' Will said, sweetly. 'But the shop ran out. So we bought popping candy instead.'

'Eh?' said Granny Maggot, bunching her grey eyebrows together. 'What in flaming cats' pyjamas does that do?'

'It pops when you put it on your tongue.'

'No Battenberg?'

'No, Gran. Just popping candy.'

'*Myergh*.'

'Can we come in?'

'*Myergh!*'

Granny Maggot shuffled back into the flat,

pouring an entire packet of popping candy directly into her mouth, which probably wasn't the best idea for a first-timer. Her cheeks practically exploded.

I nudged Will. 'Nothing's going to seem shocking after that.'

He nodded.

'We've come to take you out for the day. Isn't that nice?' Will smiled. 'Jim's idea. You remember Jim, don't you, Gran?'

Granny Maggot peered at me like I was something rotting at the back of her fridge.

'But I've just made myself a cup of tea,' she said.

'You can drink tea anytime, Gran,' Will coaxed.

'I am not going *anywhere* until I finish this cuppa, do you hear!'

We did hear, because Granny Maggot slurped

her tea very loudly. We sat down on rock-hard peach-coloured footstools, while Granny Maggot fell back into her favourite green velvet armchair. It swallowed her up like spongy moss. I wriggled with frustration (and also because my bum was aching) as Granny Maggot drank her tea. She was so slow! She sipped it, put the cup back down on the table, leant back into her chair, let out a huge sigh, then leant forward and picked it up again. Over and over. It was like some kind of tea yoga. It took forever.

We sat for a very long time in silence, my knee bouncing up and down with fear. How was I supposed to save Mrs Maggot when she was wedged into her armchair, clinging to her cup of cold tea like it was the last thing she ever planned on doing? I had to say something. But what? I couldn't just tell Granny Maggot that death was coming to get her!

'What is this muck?' grumbled Granny Maggot, struggling with her second packet of candy. 'You poisoning me or something? *Myergh!*'

'Course not, Gran,' Will sighed. 'It's –'

BANG! BANG! BANG!

'Who's that?' said Granny Maggot.

'Probably your cleaner, Gran,' Will said.

Or maybe it was Dad. A chill shot through me.

BANG!

Another knock at the door.

BANG!

And another.

BANG! BANG! BANG!

'Whoever it is really wants to come in,' Will snorted. 'Shall I go?'

Then came a voice we knew.

'Come on, Granny Maggot, I know you're in there.'

Chapter 6

'What on earth are you doing here?' Will asked.

'I've come to see Granny, blockhead,' said Will's sister.

Fiona is two years older than us, oozes cool from her head to her toes, and is so feisty she could take down a world heavyweight with a flash of her meanest look. I'm pretty sure she's part Viking.

Fiona pushed her way past us, dumped a packet of Battenberg cake on the table and crouched by Granny Maggot's armchair. 'Alright, Gran? I bought you some of that pink and yellow cake.'

'Oh, you're a sweet girl,' Granny Maggot said. Fiona was clearly her favourite. 'You didn't have to go out of your way for me.'

'It was no problem, Gran. I know how much you love Battenberg.' Fiona smiled warmly at Granny Maggot, which brought out her dimples. She's kind of fascinating, Fiona, how she can be Viking-vicious one minute and sugary-sweet the next. But don't tell anyone I said that,

okay? I don't want people to think I've spent a long time thinking about it, or anything . . .

'Er, Fiona? Can I see you in the kitchen for a minute?' I asked.

She wrinkled her nose suspiciously, like I was a talking snail or something, but followed me through to the next room. Will trailed after her.

'Oi!' Granny Maggot shouted. 'No whispering. It's rude. And if you whisper, how am I supposed to hear you?'

'So, what do you want?' spat Fiona. Back to being Viking, then . . . 'I hope you're not going to ask for my opinion on your cap, because I really have no words.'

I took it off and looked at it. It wasn't my new baseball cap at all. It was one of Mum's work caps with the words 'Happy Husk' in pink. How embarrassing! But I didn't have time to worry about that right now.

'We want to take your granny out for the day,' I said brightly.

'Yeah, Jim's doing a project on Unexpected Random Acts of Randomness,' Will informed her. 'He thinks it might improve her quality of life.'

'Wha . . .?' Her mouth hung open. I think it's a Maggot family trait.

'Jim says we should get Gran out of her routine to improve her quality of life, by doing something random.'

'Well, if anyone is going to do a project about being random, then you two are the experts,' Fiona muttered. 'So what's this got to do with me?'

'She's not really in any hurry to get out of her chair. And I need to get back to babysit my little sister later –' which was a lie, but totally necessary – 'so it has to be now.'

'And?' Fiona shook her head with impatience.

'Maybe you could persuade her?' I ventured feebly.

There was a silence while Fiona made a point of looking bored. She rolled her green eyes across the ceiling. 'Where do you want to take her?'

'I don't know – we can make it up as we go along, see what happens. An adventure.'

Fiona scuffed her foot on the floor. Then she opened her eyelids in slow motion and nodded.

'Okay, I'll come along,' she nodded. 'But only because Gran makes me laugh. I could film it. It's about time I uploaded something to my channel.'

Fiona liked posting video clips online – mainly skateboarding and scooter tricks, or people falling over. I must have watched them a thousand times (but no one knows that, okay?).

'Come on, Gran. We're going on an adventure!' Fiona said. 'Put your coat on.'

'I don't like adventures. They're boring,'
Granny Maggot moaned, but she heaved herself
to her feet. 'And what about my tea?'

'You can drink tea anytime.'

'I suppose so,' Granny Maggot tutted.

Will's shoulders dropped. 'That's what *I* said
to her,' he whispered. 'Why does she listen to
Fiona and not to me?'

'Don't worry, Will. She's probably a little bit
scared of Fiona, just like the rest of us.'

I looked up to see if Fiona had overheard me,
and that's when I spotted him through the
window. Dad. His car was pulling up outside.

'Will, let's start Gran's Big Day Out – now!'

'You're keen,' Will said, startled. He took a
step towards the front door.

'No!' I shouted. 'We're doing random things,
remember? Let's go out the back!'

'I hope your randoms get more exciting than

that,' Fiona said, fiddling with her camera phone. 'Okay, I've started filming. Let's go!'

At the back of Granny Maggot's flat was the retirement village communal garden. The really old people were sitting on benches around the edge of the lawn; in the middle more mobile old people were balancing on one leg in what seemed to be an Oldies Kung Fu lesson.

'Where you going? I hope it's the funeral home!' shouted an old man in small tight shorts and long socks who was doing the 'crane'.

'Oh shuddup, lemon lips,' Granny Maggot spat.

'Who's that?' I whispered to Fiona.

'Her best friend Arthur.' We watched Arthur stick his tongue out at Granny Maggot behind her back. 'Well, he's the best of all the enemies she's got.'

I looked behind me and saw the silhouette of

Dad in Granny Maggot's flat, scratching his head, wondering where the soon-to-be-dead old lady could be.

'Come on!' I urged. 'This isn't going to be fun unless we have speed! Lots of speed! It's time to put on a Formula Onesie!'

Granny Maggot was edging along more slowly than a well-fed sloth. It was hopeless.

Fiona let out a huge grunt. 'Do I have to do everything?'

She grabbed a chair and ran towards two old men playing chess at a garden table. She whispered something and one of them stood up, waving his arms in the air and shouting, 'WASP!' During the commotion, Fiona swapped the chair for the wheelchair and drove it back to us, one-handed. The other was still holding the camera. I tried not to be impressed, but I was. She was a pro.

We settled Granny Maggot into the wheelchair.

'You drive, I'm filming,' Fiona said, and I think Granny Maggot was even less happy than I was about that. She kept twisting around to scowl and suck her teeth at me.

'Hold tight, Granny Maggot,' I said, with an encouraging smile.

'*Myergh!*'

I looked behind. Dad was on the opposite side of the lawn, peering at everyone's faces, searching the sea of old people for his 'Client'. I gulped.

'Let's go!'

In a flash we were out of the back gates of Riverside retirement village, wheeling fast into a random adventure. Fast away from Dad. Fast away from death.

Chapter 7

Being 'on the run' was harder than it sounds because it had been raining and the pavement was full of snails.

'Oh flat-caps, there's another one!' Will exclaimed, turning round in circles. 'Someone's going to step on them. Help me, Jim! Help me save them!'

The sound of Will's snail-related agonies tore through my heart, but there was just no time for plucking the suckers off the pavement.

A dead snail was nothing compared with a dead granny. And in the distance I spotted the nose of Dad's car pulling out of Riverside car park. Three kids, a granny and a wheelchair were hard to hide on an empty pavement. If I didn't move our plan forward, the game would be up.

'Time for a random change!' I shouted. 'I'm accepting ideas. What shall we do next? Quickly! Somebody!'

'Bus,' said Fiona, calmly.

She pointed at a big double-decker chugging at a bus stop just metres away. Perfect!

The driver was just closing the folding doors, but Fiona slipped between them and stood like a starfish, holding the panels apart.

'Come on!' she shouted at us. 'Get in!'

'Oi, now hang on a minute,' the bus driver bellowed. He was a big man with one of those voices that rumbled like thunder. 'I've just finished my shift. This bus is no longer in service. Now hop it!'

'But our granny needs to get to town, and my brother needs the loo,' Fiona pleaded, sharply elbowing Will.

He got the hint and did a panicky little toilet dance, which involved flapping his hands and hopping on the spot. Until there was a crunch under his foot. Will completely lost it then, crumpling to the pavement and wailing.

'Seriously?' muttered Fiona, shaking her head. 'Look, driver, we're getting on whether you like it or not. Consider yourself hijacked.'

The driver puffed out his chest, which made the buttons on his shirt strain. No one said anything for a moment and the air was so still the crinkling of a Curly-Wurly wrapper would have sounded like gunfire. 'Now look here, if you don't move I'll report –'

'I want Battenberg, I'm hungry!' shouted Granny Maggot.

The bus driver leaned forward to look at her. He softened and grinned. 'What was that, dearie?'

'Battenberg! Stop off somewhere that sells Battenberg,' Granny Maggot repeated. She leapt out of the wheelchair, flashed her old person's free bus pass and climbed aboard. 'And Will, bring that chair thing,' she said over her shoulder. 'I've had my eye on Stanley's wheels for ages.' She cackled.

Luckily for us the driver burst into hoots of laughter so Will and I jumped on, pulling the wheelchair after us. The closing doors knocked my Happy Husk hat off into the gutter, which was probably a good thing.

'Oh,' he said, when he noticed we were all aboard. 'So you *have* hijacked me? Well, you can't make me drive.'

'Please?' I begged.

Will sniffed next to me. He had tears in his eyes. Probably because he'd squashed a snail, which is against his religion as a mollusc-lover. I looked at Fiona, who usually had all the bright ideas, but she was busy filming her granny, who was directly accusing the bus seats of being too brightly coloured.

'Give me one good reason,' the driver challenged.

I looked behind the bus and down the road. I could see Dad's car caught at traffic lights, but he wouldn't be there for long. I had to tell the bus driver something. So I whispered a little half-truth in his ear.

'Oh, I am very sorry to hear that!' the driver exclaimed, swallowing my story. He jabbed a thumb in the direction of Granny Maggot, who had taken to slapping the seats to punish them. 'Is she suffering, or is she always like this?'

'No, she's always like this, actually,' I said. 'But my mate, well, he really loves her anyway.'

'And love makes the world go round,' the bus driver replied, with a deep sigh. 'Well, I'll tell you what – I have to get this big old bus back to the station and I don't suppose there's any reason why I shouldn't give you a lift. Especially seeing as you've reminded me about the tenderness of love.'

'Great. Thank you. But we need to go now, and go fast,' I said politely but hurriedly. 'We want her day out to be extra exciting, and Mrs Maggot's a secret speed freak!' I added in a whisper.

'No problems, son. I was a rally driver before I was a bus driver.'

'Were you really?'

'Well, in my dreams.' He grinned a little crazily. Now, I *am* a bit of speed freak, but I like speed when it's me in control on my scooter – not when it's a double-decker bus driven by a pretend rally driver easily distracted by thoughts of love and tenderness. 'Right,' he called to everyone, 'are you all seated? It's time we went broom-broom.'

The bus driver licked his fingers and ran them through his eyebrows, a determined expression on his face. Maybe our sticky situation had just got even stickier.

Double-decker buses have a tendency to make me feel a little car sick at the best of times. Right now our bus driver was in rally mode and seemed to have forgotten the brakes entirely. We were swaying and swerving across the road and with every corner the bus swung wildly. Each time this happened Granny Maggot shouted 'Myergh!', Fiona growled because it jolted her camera, and Will – who was still looking pale about the crushed snail – toppled this way and that way. I started to feel really sick, not just with the motion of the bus, but with the realisation of what I was doing. Everything had happened so quickly, from finding out about the *DADS*, to working out what it meant and then kidnapping Granny Maggot. I sat down by the window, closed my eyes and breathed deeply. I needed to find my inner strength and stay calm. And I needed to make sure Dad didn't find out. If he did . . .

Okay, so now seems like a good time to tell you about memory wiping – and how Will once knew my Dad was Death. You see, Will was with me when I walked the creepy corridors of The Dead End Office in search of the truth about Dad; Will was there when the truth came out, when Dad admitted that he wasn't an accountant – that he was in charge of Natural Deaths in Greater London. But now he doesn't remember anything about it. Dad wiped his memory. That day Dad could have wiped my memory, too, but I begged him not to and said he could trust me. And he did. I'll say it again: trust is a big thing between me and Dad, and if I broke that trust, if he found out what I was up to . . . The thought was more crushing than a herd of buffalo on a snail-infested pavement.

'Jim! Jim!'

My eyes sprung open to see Will's eyes

millimetres from mine, wide and bright. He was panting like an old Labrador and his hair was ruffled as if he'd just spent the night in a hay barn.

'Jim, you've got to see this!'

He tugged my arm so hard I fell onto the floor of the bus. The bus was swinging round a particularly big bend, so I couldn't get to my feet again and I floundered around like a donkey on an ice rink. Then I heard laughter – a series of loud cackles, like seagulls fighting over a crisp packet. Probably Fiona, laughing at me.

Will pulled me to my feet. 'Can you believe it?' he asked.

Fiona was laughing, but not at me. Granny Maggot was standing up, holding tight to one of the bars, giggling like mad every time the bus swayed. She looked like a happy orangutan, but with shorter arms.

'Wheeeeeee!'

    . . . Whoosh!'

       . . . THIS IS BETTER THAN
BATTENBERG!'

Fiona was filming it all on her camera phone. She was grinning ear to ear – with dimples and everything – and it must have been catching, because within seconds I was smiling, too. Fiona shouted for the bus to go faster and turn more corners, which the bus driver was really happy to do because it made him feel even more like a rally driver.

'Easy left! Hard right! Vroom-vroom,' he shouted, before laughing heartily. Soon I was crying with laughter alongside the others. Maybe Granny Maggot's unusual joyfulness was a sign that the HEX machine had got it wrong. She seemed so happy! If her death date

were a mistake, my mission to save her was
more important than ever.

'Whooopeeee!' Granny Maggot bellowed.

'BETTER THAN BATTENBERG!' we all
shouted back. Which was a bit spooky, as we
hadn't rehearsed that.

Chapter 8

Granny Maggot's good mood disappeared when we stopped at the bus station in town. Even if we could keep on driving, I'm not sure our stomachs were up for any more of Kevin's corners. I did try to explain that to her, but she started stamping her feet and punching the air. Looking after Granny Maggot was kind of like babysitting a chimpanzee – funny, until the bananas run out . . .

'*MYERGH!*' she shouted, as she got out of the bus. '*Myergh!*'

We had to get moving, and not just because of the lack of bananas. The bus station was full of people – jam packed – and the last thing we needed was a crowd to slow us down if Dad turned up. I didn't know where he was and that made me nervous. Did he see us get on the bus? Had he followed us into town? Was he going to pounce at any moment?

'Hey, everyone,' I called, but no one was listening. Fiona was checking her film, Granny was muttering, the bus driver was fiddling with his keys and Will was checking the bottom of his shoe. I started to feel panicky – panicky about getting stuck, and panicky that, as a pretty strange collection of people, we'd draw attention. All it would take was one of Dad's colleagues to see us, and you don't need to be good at maths to see how that would add up – *Jim was with Granny Maggot, who should be dead. Suspicious!* I was in charge of this adventure, and I needed to make a stand.

'Look, I need to make a stand,' I said boldly.

Will suddenly pulled an old crate from a pile of rubbish in the terminal and turned it upside down.

'I made one for you!' he said, standing on it to test out its strength. He wasn't even laughing. It wasn't a joke. Now you can see what I have to deal with.

'No, Will. I need to say something.'

'SOMETHING,' he shouted, quickly. This time he *was* laughing. The hysterical episode on the bus must have altered his brain chemistry. But at least he wasn't crying over a snail.

'I need to say something serious,' I tried.

'SOMETHING SERIOUS,' he interrupted,

sniggering into his sleeve. I think I preferred it when he was crying over a snail.

'Oh my gawd,' Fiona moaned. 'You are both so unfunny. I think I'm calling it a day.' She shoved her phone in her jacket pocket.

'But what about Granny Maggot?' I said quickly. 'We can't be responsible for her all on our own . . . She only listens to you!'

This point was true, although I also didn't want Fiona to go, because, well, you know . . .

'Alright, I'll help you get her home, then,' Fiona said. 'Then I'm off.'

'We can't go back to Riverside,' I said quickly. 'Not, um, until we've finished the Unexpected Random Acts of Randomness experiment.'

'How much longer will it take?' she sighed.

'Not long,' I lied.

'Can't trust you two to put your pants on the right way round,' she grumbled.

Will pulled the elastic on his pants to check for a label – but a thought gripped him and he let go, with a painful snap.

'How are you calculating the results of the Unexpected Random Acts of Randomness experiment?' he asked, adjusting his glasses.

'Yeah,' Fiona said, turning her green eyes on me. 'What are the results so far?'

'So far? . . . I can conclude that, er, that so far it looks as if getting out and about unexpectedly is quite a good thing for improving quality of life,' I replied, though my voice got higher at the end, which made me sound a bit shaky.

Will shook his head slowly. 'That's very poor science, Jim. When I measure things, there's usually some sort of ruler involved. Or at least a comparison – like "This peanut is BIGGER than that peanut . . ."'

'I have never been MORE BORED,' Fiona moaned.

'Hang on,' I tried, wanting to please both of them. 'What about the bit on the bus when we all shouted "better than Battenberg"? It was BETTER than Battenberg. And it was fun, wasn't it? Granny Maggot thought it was, didn't you . . . Mrs Maggot?'

The wheelchair and the granny were gone. 'Er, where *is* Gran?' asked Will.

We eventually found Granny Maggot and her new friend, the bus driver, outside a supermarket, scoffing Battenberg cake and cheesy Wotsits.

'Granny,' Fiona panted. 'What are you doing?'

'What does it look like?' she muttered, spraying orange, pink and yellow crumbs.

'Wotsit look like!' laughed the bus driver. 'Good one, Sally.'

Sally? We looked at each other. No one had called Mrs Maggot by her first name since Will's grandpa died.

'We're having a food adventure,' said Granny Maggot, stuffing a chunk of cake into her gob with one hand and a clutch of crisps with the other. 'A terrific food adventure! And why not, seeing as I'm about to die . . .'

'You're about to die!' Will and Fiona exclaimed.

'Yes, and you know it. Kevin told me what you said. So the doctor says I'm on my last legs and it might be my last day out? You rats! Didn't even have the guts to come out and tell me yourselves. Disgraceful way to treat your own gran.'

'What?' Will started . . .

'I just made that up!' I jumped in. 'To get us on the bus. Granny Maggot's not going to die, look at her! She's full of life. It's not your last day, Mrs Maggot. Not at all. I bet you it's not! Who would think there was a day to die. Not me. I'd never . . .'

There was a strange silence, and I felt as if I'd gone over the top. Will put his face up close to mine and peered at me through his frames.

'Your face,' he said.

I gulped. Did my expression give me away? Did they all see through the double bluff? How would I explain it? Fiona moved closer, too, so her nose was almost touching my cheek. I held my breath.

'Oh that is *gross*!' she said.

Did she mean my face? Will laughed. 'It's just a little spider, Jim . . . I thought it was a bit of Wotsit until it started moving.'

The bus driver leaned forward to brush the spider off my face with his very Wotsity finger.

'Mr Bus Driver –' I protested, as he smeared orange paste across my face.

'His name's Kevin, you imbecile,' Granny Maggot scolded. 'And we're spending the day together.'

Kevin casually shrugged, as if he had no choice in the matter and was happy that way. He popped open another bag of Wotsits.

'I thought your shift was over and it was time to go home?' Will said.

Kevin just chuckled and shrugged again.

'Isn't there anything else you should be doing, Kevin?' asked Fiona, impatiently. 'Some place you need to be? Family, friends . . .?'

'Nope. No family left. And I have pledged to act on your grandmother's every whim today. Just say the word, Sally Magic, and it shall be done.'

'The name's Maggot,' Fiona said.

'Well, she's magic to me.'

'I DON'T WANT TO GO HOME!' Granny Maggot hissed, leaping from the wheelchair with her hands clenched in angry fists. 'I want to go to the park. The big one!'

'Then, Sally Magic, that is where we'll go. Back to the rally bus! No one will notice if we borrow it for a bit longer, will they?' he chuckled.

Kevin briskly wheeled Granny Maggot away.

Fiona surrendered, throwing her arms in the air. 'We can't let a total stranger take our granny to the park!'

'He might run off with her. They might go to Scotland and get married and we'd never see her again,' Will insisted. 'We can't lose her!' Tears were already springing to his eyes.

You won't lose her, Will, I said to myself. *I'll make sure of that.*

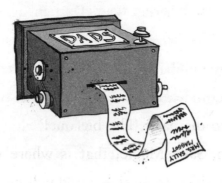

Chapter 9

Mrs Maggot insisted on taking Stanley's stolen wheelchair to the park. Getting it on and off the bus was a pain (it was heavy and awkward) but it was probably for the best. The country park is enormous – made up of woodlands and fields – and a granny on wheels was going to be much faster than a granny on foot if we found ourselves in a hasty get-away situation.

I had high hopes there wouldn't be one,

though, as I hadn't seen Dad in ages; I was pretty sure we'd given him the slip. The stretched rubber-band feeling relaxed as we walked and wheeled up and down the pathways that criss-crossed the parklands, chatting like it was any regular day out. Kevin shared his stories about bus driving, Will told us how we was going to complain to the editor of *Snail Enthusiast Monthly* about its unfairly scathing article about ramshorn snails, and Granny Maggot made jokes. Who knew she had so many? We all agreed our favourite one was: 'Why do squirrels swim on their backs? To keep their nuts dry!' It made us laugh so much that Kevin had to go and stand on his own behind a tree to calm down, and Fiona's film went all shaky. When she laughed she made these little soft snorts, like kitten sneezes . . . It was easy to forget why we were here.

At the duck pond, Kevin, Fiona and I sat on a bench. Granny Maggot wheeled herself over to the water's edge, and made clucking noises at the pigeons and ducks. They waddled close to peck crumbs of cake and crisps that had fallen from her lap and she sighed, over and over.

'You okay, Gran?' Fiona called.

'Okay?' she hollered back. 'I'm more than okay. Why haven't you ever taken me to feed the ducks before, eh? Visiting me in that rat-cage of a room . . . Bet you were bored out of your heads doing granny duty. Silly sausages. From now on, we'll be getting out in the open, right? No more stuffy old rooms and boring conversations about school and boyfriends and what your mum and dad are up to.' She pointed at Fiona and waggled her finger. And then she pointed at me. 'Maybe you should listen to your little mate, and take me out more often.'

Fiona shot me a look I couldn't read – but I hoped it was admiration. Will fell to his knees.

'Sorry, Gran, I had no idea you were interested in the outside world. I should have thought of it before. I'm terrible. I'm a terrible person.'

'*Myergh*,' she said, but her face was soft. 'You're my grandson and I won't allow anyone to be rude about my grandson, not even you!' Then, amazingly, she jumped up from her wheelchair, walked over to Will and rubbed his cheek with affection. 'Not your fault. You're just a little boy. Come feed the ducks with me.'

Will practically melted on the spot. It was

the kind of scene we needed to stop and appreciate, but it looked as if we wouldn't have the luxury for cherishing special moments. Dad's car had just come into view and my rubber band snapped tight again. We were conveniently hidden by the bushes and trees around the pond, and I watched as his car followed the road which led to the car park at the very top of the park.

We'd be safe for a while but I had to stay alert.

Dad was obviously planning to search the park, though, so I rummaged in my rucksack for the binoculars, and kept watch. While the others made quacking noises and told squirrel jokes, I scanned the park above us, silent and a bit sweaty with apprehension. It was as if they were all actors in a sit-com while I was starring in a spy film.

Then it became a thriller.

A figure I recognised appeared at the top of the next field. Dad. He was walking in our direction, diagonally across the grass, looking left and right, sometimes turning full circle to check behind him. He was searching. He was *hunting*. If he got too much closer, it would be too close for comfort. Maybe he had his own binoculars. Who knows – maybe he didn't need them, because maybe there was an Eye Training room at The Dead End Office . . . I couldn't take the chance.

'Better move on, now, everyone,' I said, forcing a cheery smile.

'Why?' Fiona asked.

'Because we just should.' I clapped my hands. It was supposed to be for encouragement but it scared the ducks into the air. They shot up, dropping feathers and poo.

'Now look what you've done!' Granny Maggot squawked.

'Jim!' Will exclaimed disapprovingly. 'That was mean.'

'Yes, well, sorry. But the ducks have gone now, so maybe we could leave.'

'Why are you in such a rush?' Will quizzed.

'Well, because Fiona wanted to film something funny and we're just standing here and doing nothing . . . And also this isn't random enough! We need to be random and unexpected for the project or it won't work. This is our last chance . . .' I tailed off.

They were looking at me as if I had spidery Wotsit crumbs all over my face.

I looked over Will's shoulder at the approaching figure of my father. The Grim Reaper. I clenched my fists and thought at a hundred miles an hour. But my brain had stalled.

'If you're bored, you can go home,' Will said.

'What?'

'This is supposed to be Granny Maggot's day out, and she wants to stay here. If she wants to stay, then we're staying. Because that's what she wants to do.'

'But I think we should all do something else now!' I said, slightly hysterically. 'The project!'

'The project doesn't matter, Jim,' Will sighed. 'For a start, it doesn't seem to me as if you've thought it through properly. And anyway, I've changed my mind. I want to spend the day with Gran. Your project can wait. It's hardly a matter of life and death.'

I lifted my binoculars and pointed them towards Dad. Maybe it was the flustered ducks that had caught his attention, but he was now looking straight at us with interest. Even if he couldn't recognise our faces from that far away, the wheelchair would surely give us away.

I realised this could go one of two ways:

1) I could stay: *I'd be in trouble.*
2) I could leave, but Will might innocently tell him about my 'project': *I'd be in trouble.*

It was no good. I was between a rock and a hard place, I was caught in a trap, I was done for, I was cornered, I was . . . *getting wet?*

A large raindrop plopped onto my nose. Then another. I gasped.

'It's raining!' I cried happily. 'It's raining!'

Chapter 10

Granny Maggot hated rain and started on the *myerghs* again.

Kevin told her, 'Just say the word,' and Granny Maggot said: 'Go!' So that's what we did. We wheeled her like crazy down the hill and onto Kevin's bus (which he'd illegally parked in a bus stop).

I put my binoculars against the window of the glass. Dad was by the pond, turning in circles, getting wet. I felt a bit bad about that.

'You really like looking for birds all of a sudden,' Will said, sitting next to me. 'Do you know what I think is weird about binoculars? The unnecessary N. *Bi* means two and *ocular* means eye. What's the meaning of the *N*? There are lots of unnecessary Ns in English. Binocular. Column. Autumn. Condemn . . .'

'Where are we going now?' Kevin said, turning on the engine and saving me from the deep end of Will's spelling mysteries. 'Back to Riverside?'

I looked at old Sally Maggot. Her head had started to nod forward. If she said she wanted to go home, how would I stop her? We needed to keep her happy. We needed 'bananas'.

'Urgh! My phone's wet,' Fiona moaned, slumping against the seat.

I didn't have a tissue – but I wanted to make a show of trying. Just so she'd see I cared. I patted my pockets. The left one crinkled. I pushed my hand in and brought out a piece of paper. It said:

Give and Tak contact
Hetty gav Jim sizzers, so
Jim haz to giv Hetty swits

I stared at it, trying to decode the awful spelling. *Give and Take Contract.* Of course. And I could see where this was going. In return for giving me the scissors, Hetty wanted something back. Swits? Ah! *Sweets.* Hetty wanted sweets. And who could blame her? Mum said all the sugar and E-numbers in sweets made kids go crazy and unable to sleep, so she never bought them for us. Unless we were in shock.

'You got a tissue or not?' Fiona said.

'Er, no, sorry,' I said, slightly distracted. I was thinking about all the sugar and E-numbers that made you unable to sleep.

'Riverside, Sally? Just say the word,' Kevin called.

'Would you mind if we stopped off on the way?' I said. 'A day out wouldn't be a day out without sweets. And I know a newsagent that stocks *Rally Extreme Magazine*. I'd like to get it for you, Kevin. To say thank you.'

Bingo!

Streets the Newsagent does sell *Rally Extreme*, and it is also the best sweet shop in the world. It has all the normal chocolate bars and stuff, but it also has rows and rows of gummies, fizzies, sours and chewies. You can buy just one, or you can fill a whole bag. Will and I go there every Tuesday on the way to school.

That's when they have their crisps delivery (and I just love fresh crisps). The trouble is, Streets is just around the corner from where I live. It's dangerously close to home, so at any point Mum, Dad or a neighbour could walk in. Going there would be a huge risk. Unless you're the world's best crisps consumer.

I might not have been the biggest crisp eater in the whole wide world, but I was pretty sure I was the best crisps customer Streets the Newsagent had ever had. So I didn't feel bad about asking the owner, Mrs Davis, to close her shop for two minutes while we chose our pick 'n' mix.

'Why?' she asked. 'It's a shop. And shops stay open so people can come in and out of them. Unless you're the Queen, I am not shutting the shop for you.'

'It needs to be a very private sweet sale,' I

insisted. 'We don't want people to see us buying sweets.'

'Nothing wrong with a couple of sweets,' she laughed. 'A little of what you fancy does you good.'

'But we're not buying a little of what we fancy,' I said, mischievously. 'We're buying a lot of what we fancy. There's five of us.' I winked. I thought it might look good.

The thought of a large sweet sale went down well. I called for the others to get off the bus and Mrs Davis ushered them into the tiny shop (the wheelchair had to stay behind), and flicked the *Open* sign to *Closed*. She gave us extra large pick 'n' mix bags and told us to help ourselves.

'To anything?' Granny Maggot said, eyeing the trays of sweets.

'Anything at all. As much as you want!' Mrs Davis smiled. 'You pay by weight, not by sweet. So fill 'em bags up!'

There was a furious pouring of sour cherries, cola bottles and liquorice laces and the air twinkled with sugar dust. Some of it landed on Granny Maggot's lips and her tongue flicked out, quick as a lizard.

'Myergh!' she said.

Then: 'Myeeeerm.'

Then: '*Myum* . . .' Her voice got perkier and perkier.

'Look, there's some of that popping candy over there,' Will pointed. 'And gummy sweets. They're my favourite.'

'It's not Battenberg,' Granny Maggot mumbled, quite happily grabbing a handful of gummy snakes.

Fiona took a photo: Granny Maggot's mouth

was dripping with snakes like she was some sort of deep-sea monster.

'That is priceless,' she laughed. But I knew, technically, it wasn't – and paying for all this was going to be a real issue. And there was *Rally Extreme*. Reading for rally enthusiasts didn't come cheap.

'That'll be £25.17p,' Mrs Davis announced gleefully, when we'd totted it all up. There were bulging bags of sweets for everyone (including Hetty).

'Please could you give me a bill?' I asked. 'I'll come back and pay for it later. I only live round the corner.'

Mrs Davis agreed, but said if I didn't then she'd ring my parents, and she made me write down my telephone number and address. I decided to worry about that later.

'Jim? Could you come out here a minute?'

Will's voice was a bit shaky, but that's not what made me run to the door. It was the shouts of 'Watch it!' and 'Steady on' and 'BLEEDIN' HELL, GET THAT GRANNY IN A CAGE!'

Granny Maggot's knees were no longer playing up – she had skipped out of the shop and was zigzagging up and down the pavement outside, pinching the bottoms of passers-by. Mum was right, E-numbers did drive you loopy. This was a sugar rush like nothing I'd ever seen before. And the sweets weren't just keeping Granny Maggot awake – they were making her totally hyperactive.

'She's having fun,' chuckled Kevin, leaning against a lamppost with his hands crossed over his chest.

'This is wicked!' Fiona grinned, chewing on Brain-Sparks candy and following Granny Maggot with her camera.

No it wasn't. It was *disastrous*. We needed to keep a low profile! I had to think of something quickly. 'Stop her, she's a menace to society!' I shouted. Fiona and Kevin looked at me funnily. I'd gone over the top again, I had to stop doing that. I breathed deeply and turned to Will. 'We need to calm your gran down before she hurts herself,' I said. 'We don't want "going to hospital" to be one of our random adventures, do we?'

'Granny in hospital? I couldn't bear it,' Will said, looking shocked at the thought.

Granny Maggot was trying to leapfrog a bollard.

'Kevin, grab her, will you?' I said. 'Before something terrible happens.'

To Will or Kevin a broken foot would be 'something terrible', but I knew of a far greater danger. And I'd just noticed his car parked further down the street. Dad was here again. How did he keep finding us?

'Kevin, please!' I shouted.

Kevin caught Mrs Maggot mid-leap and carried her onto the bus, where she continued to swing like a baboon from the handrails and zoom up and down the aisle, using the wheelchair as a scooter. But it wasn't funny any more. Funny things don't stay funny forever, no matter how funny they are. But Granny Maggot had a year's worth of sugar inside her and it didn't look as if she was going to calm down any time soon. The bus was rocking from side to side.

'I can't drive like this,' Kevin chuckled, although he was starting to look a little concerned. 'If the police see me I'll be in real trouble.'

'Well, we can't take her to Riverside,' I said.

'Not like this. She'll trash her flat!' (I was pleased with that.)

'Or kung fu Arthur in the backside!' Fiona laughed.

'What are we going to do?' Will squealed.

'We have got to get her somewhere where she can burn off energy without making a complete song and dance –' I stopped and looked at Will. 'Your house is just round the corner.'

'We don't have any energy-burning equipment,' Will frowned.

'No, but you do have your mum,' I grinned.

Chapter 11

Will lives in a terraced road, where the houses are joined together and everyone likes to know everything that's going on. We parked the big red bus outside Number 16, and all the neighbours squashed their faces against their windows to get a look at us as we got off.

'Where are we?' said Granny Maggot, staring back at them with disgust. 'The zoo?'

There was an explosion of music as Fiona opened the front door of their house.

'Fiona, that you, love?' came a voice down the hall.

'Yes, Mum. And we've brought visitors!'

'Guests? Well, bring them in, bring them in!' the voice cried.

We shuffled down the corridor into the kitchen – Fiona, Will, me, Kevin, and behind Kevin, Granny Maggot. Will's mum was holding a dishcloth and dancing to pop music on the radio. She's always dancing. She's like one of those flowerpot toys that bop every time there's a sound. Basically, she's a bit bananas. And just what we needed.

'Hello, Jim Wimple,' she said, smiling at me. She always calls me by my full name.

'This is Kevin,' Will said, pointing at the bus driver, who was so large that somehow Will's mum hadn't even noticed him. Like he was part of the house or something.

'Pleased to meet you, Mrs Maggot,' he said, licking his fingers and smoothing his eyebrows.

'And we've got a surprise for you, Mum,' said Fiona. Kevin stood aside.

'Sally!' Will's mum cried – the second Sally of the day! – and she wrapped her arms around the old lady. 'Oh my goodness, this calls for a cup of tea!'

Granny Maggot didn't seem to want to let go of Will's mum, so they just did a rocking hug on the spot.

'Oh, stuff the cup of tea! This calls for a party!' Will's mum said, breaking away. She pushed back all the furniture and turned up the volume on the radio. 'Who's for a bit of "Dancing Queen"? Can't listen to Abba and not dance, can you!'

Actually, it's not just Abba – Will's mum can't not dance to anything. If the only sound in the house was a ticking clock, she'd be jumping or jiggling and making her bangles rattle. Will's mum hit the 'dance floor' in the middle of the tiny kitchen, and fluttered her hands at Granny Maggot, who grasped them and stepped forward.

'If disco moves are too much, love, then just do air guitar,' Will's mum advised.

'Come on, Sally Magic, I'll take the lead,' boomed Kevin, who didn't look quite right dancing to Abba, but definitely deserved points for enthusiasm.

There wasn't much room left for the rest of us to dance, which was probably for the best, because Fiona got out her phone to film us again and I didn't want to look like an idiot in front of her. For lots of reasons, but mainly because Fiona isn't kind to idiots. (A photo of Will with his trousers on back-to-front didn't

make its way round school on its own, that's all I'm saying . . .)

A song called 'Oops Upside Your Head' came on and Will's mum went wild. Kevin jumped, which made the teacups rattle on the shelf, and Granny Maggot punched her little fists in the air. Fiona was filming like crazy. Will had his fingers in his ears.

'Want to check on Maximus?' he mouthed.

I nodded.

Maximus is Will's giant African land snail. It sleeps most of the time, but Will woke it up with a warm soak in the bathroom sink. The snail slowly unfurled itself, dragging out its head from where it was tucked, deep inside its shell, behind its own bottom. Its eyes and feelers rolled out and wavered, testing the air around it. Maximus is a pretty awesome creature, it has to be said. Not awesome enough to be stared at for hours, though, like Will does. Once he spent an entire weekend watching Maximus, only taking breaks to sleep and pee.

'Do you know that an *Achatina achatina* African land snail once grew to fifteen inches?' Will told me. 'That's longer than a ruler.'

'Imagine measuring things with your snail at school,' I said, laughing. 'What if Mr Curlewis said "measure the length of these lines" and then you got out Maximus, all slimy . . .' I snorted at the thought of Mr Curlewis's, face, but Will was thinking, so his ears weren't working. Parts of his body often shut down when he's really focused on a particular thought or idea.

'Maximus is an *Achatina fulica*, so he wouldn't grow as long as a ruler and you wouldn't get a precise measurement. But there is one measurement you can take with him . . .' Will looked me in the eye. He paused for effect. 'How much do I love Maximus, Jim?'

'You love him a lot. Loads. Heaps. Your love for Maximus is deeper than the ocean.'

'Yes. And I love Granny Maggot more than that. So there you have a pretty good measurement of how much I love my granny.'

I shifted uncomfortably. 'Why are you telling me that?'

'Because I want you to know how much today means to me, Jim. I'm having the best day with Gran – just the best. She's only spat at me twice so far, and even then I think it's only because her dentures were slipping. And it's thanks to you and your Unexpected Random Acts of Randomness experiment. I'm sorry I doubted you.'

He put his hand on mine, which was a nice gesture. Shame it was covered in giant African land snail slime.

The music downstairs suddenly turned off. Music never gets turned off in the Maggot house . . . not unless it's something serious, like the neighbours complaining. Could my dad have found us?

We crept downstairs to see what was up. Will's mum was on the phone.

'Oh right . . .' she was saying, trying to sound casual. 'Alright, love,' she said. 'See you in a bit.' She put the phone down and turned to face us. 'Dicky's knocked off early. He'll be home in half an hour.'

'C'mon, Gran, let's get you back on the bus,' Fiona said, snapping into action.

'I've got your coat, Gran,' said Will.

'What's going on?' I said, resisting the push towards the front door.

'It's our dad. He's coming home early from work at the garage. He and Granny Maggot don't speak much,' Fiona said.

'He doesn't speak to me, more like,' Mrs

Maggot tutted. 'He's a big boy now. He should get over it and give his mum some respect.'

'Now's not the time, Gran,' Fiona said. 'He's always grumpy after work. Starving, usually. So it's probably best if we left making up for another day.'

'Why don't your dad and Mrs Maggot speak?' I asked Will, as we headed for the door.

'She sold his entire Lego collection. Thirty years ago.'

'Bet you can't measure that with a snail, Will,' I said.

'*Achatina fulica* live for around thirty years, so you probably could, actually,' Will said, at my side. 'The whole world is connected, Jim.'

Some things aren't worth arguing about.

'It's so silly, so silly,' Mrs Maggot tutted. 'He's my little boy . . .'

'You should probably get her back to

Riverside, anyway,' Will's mum said, leaning forward to dab Granny Maggot's sweaty brow. 'She's probably had enough excitement for today. Have you, love?' she said, putting her arm around the old lady's shoulders. 'Is it time to go home?'

Mrs Maggot was a bit out of breath and her face had fallen from Abba-happy into the abyss of weariness. She looked kind of sad, too. I wondered if it was because she regretted selling the Lego.

'I'll get her home right away,' Kevin said, circling Granny Maggot's shoulders with his huge arm. 'I'll make sure she gets into her favourite armchair with a nice cup of tea.'

'It's been lovely to see you.' Will's mum gave Granny Maggot a little squeeze.

'Say hello to Dicky for me, won't you,' Granny Maggot said, hopefully. She wiped a tear from her eye. Kevin handed her a Wotsity handkerchief.

'I will,' said Will's mum with a meek smile. 'And I'll pop down to Riverside soon, okay? Soon as I can get away. Bring you some of that funny-coloured cake you like.'

The mention of cake made my tummy rumble, but as I was bustled out, Will's mum pressed some cold pizza into my hand. She knows I love pizza.

'Bye, Jim Wimple, love,' she said as the front door closed. It was the second time she'd saved my skin that afternoon.

Chapter 12

Kevin said he needed a pee and popped back inside while the rest of us settled back on the bus. Fiona stretched out on a row of seats, snorting as she replayed the film of her granny doing air guitar. Will took a seat next to Granny Maggot. He held her hand and pointed at things out of the window. She didn't say *myergh* once. But I could tell by the way her eyelids kept drooping she was tired. She was ready for a lie down. But if we went back to Riverside she'd be having a very long lie down indeed, and Will would be feeling a grief that was deeper than the deepest part of the ocean, unmeasurable even by the colossal squid (which is the largest member of the mollusc family).

But Granny Maggot was totally pooped. I'd run out of ideas. There was nothing I could do now. It was out of my hands.

Close to tears, I climbed to the top deck of the bus so I wouldn't have to watch my best friend and his favourite granny enjoying each other's company, when I knew it was for the last time. The guilt was killing me.

I once read that when astronauts look back down on our planet and see how small it is, they have these moments of clear thinking. They think things like 'What's important about hating broccoli and not doing homework and missing a penalty shot on a little planet called Earth, when there's a gazillion stars on fire and universe that has no end?'

I began to feel a bit like those astronauts. Okay, I wasn't in orbit, but being on the top deck seemed to put things in perspective and what I realised was this: I was trying to do my best for Will and make Fiona like me and keep my promise to Dad . . . But I was missing the point. The point was, a life was about to be taken – extinguished like a flame being snuffed out – and it wasn't out of my hands at all. In fact, everything was *in* my hands. And how many kids get to say that – *I can stop Death*? None. Just me. Giving up now would be wasting opportunities, throwing away powers and privileges. Trust was a big thing between me and Dad, but when I looked at the big picture – at the universe and saving grannies not ready to die – it seemed a small sacrifice.

If I stopped worrying about what trouble I'd get into I could do something great. Something incredible. I could keep Granny Maggot alive! But it was time I had an accomplice.

Will ran at lightning speed up the bus stairs.

'Where is it?' he panted. 'It sounds like a slim snaggletooth! But they're usually found in Florida, not London!'

'Will, there is no snail,' I admitted. 'I made it up. I just wanted you to come up here.'

'But snaggletooths *do* look like pasta coils. You can't make that up.'

'Well, I did.'

'How disappointing,' Will said. 'I'm going back down to Gran.'

'Will, I have something to tell you.' I patted the seat next to me. 'An incredible fact.'

Will stopped and adjusted his glasses. 'Aliens landed on your roof again?'

'No, but you might want to sit down, anyway.'

And that's when I told him the truth about Dad's job. And Will said *cool* a lot and did some gory miming. He just wasn't taking it seriously – but he would when I told him the full story. And it was time I did.

'Will,' I said, grabbing his hand (to stop him pretend-stabbing his guts again). 'He's going to get Granny Maggot.'

'Ha ha! Good one!' he said.

Will can't process lies. Even lies that are joke lies. So I'd never say 'you've got bird poo on your head' if he didn't. He wouldn't understand. It would melt his marshmallow. I just wouldn't do it . . . So the possibility of Will not believing me had never crossed my mind.

'It's not a joke, Will,' I said through clenched teeth.

'Oh, you're good,' Will snorted, nodding. He clapped his hands.

'I'm not kidding,' I said in my most serious voice, and I tried out Dad's scariest face – The Cold Eye – for effect. I held my head high, looking down my nose in a terrifying stare with eyes ready to pierce like laser beams.

'You look like a startled meerkat,' Will said. 'Are you feeling alright?'

Suddenly the bus tilted. Kevin had finished his pee and was boarding. The engine started and we pulled away. We were on our way to Riverside. I had to persuade Will I was telling the truth.

'We need to go to my house,' I said. 'Right

now. I've got something to show you. It's important.'

'Promise you won't do that meerkat thing?' Will said, unsure. 'That freaked me out.'

'I promise.'

But if an unintentional meerkat impression freaked him out, just imagine how he'd feel when he saw his granny's name on the tickertape of death.

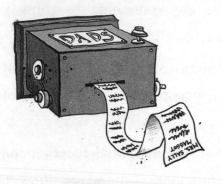

Chapter 13

We ran down to the lower deck of the bus and told Kevin we wanted to make a detour. He said he was okay with that, because he was waiting for a call and wanted to 'drive around a bit' before going to Riverside, which we thought was a bit weird, but suited us fine.

My house was just round the corner. I live in a road of semi-detached houses, and it's much less friendly than Will's road. People are equally nosy, though, and are usually looking out for reasons to report you to the council. A bus stopping at the side of the road would definitely be something to moan about. So Will and I hopped off and told Kevin to go round the block a couple of times.

I realised that if Dad was home, having Will with me might complicate things. Dad might suspect something. So I told Will to hide in the front garden while I checked the house. Actually, what I really said was that I'd seen those snails in the shape of pasta coils in the front bushes.

I left him scouring the front bushes for snails and walked into the kitchen. Hetty was stirring orange juice in a mixing bowl. Mum was kneading the orange peel with something brown on the counter.

'Oh, Jim!' Mum flustered, when she saw me. 'Where have you been?'

'I went to the skate park,' I lied.

'He's been with Will,' Hetty said. 'I followed you up the road earlier.'

'Yeah . . . but,' I stumbled, grimacing at Hetty, 'Will had to go and see his granny, so I went the skate park on my own.'

'Is that true?' Hetty narrowed her eyes. I gave her a peek of the bag of sweets behind my back. She lit up like a Christmas tree. 'Yep, it's true!' she said, hopping off her stool. She gave me a hug, grabbed the sweets and ran upstairs, whooping.

'No matter, you're here now,' Mum said. 'And I want you try some of my raw orange, carrot and beetroot cake.' I opened my mouth to object, but Mum popped a slice of goo right on my tongue. Totally ruined the flavour of Will's mum's pizza slice. 'It might be a bit gloopy – my hand slipped when pouring in the chia seeds. But the flavour's good, hmmm?'

'Grrmmmmm.' I couldn't talk – my teeth were glued together.

'I knew it was a good one,' Mum smiled, pinching my cheek. 'Maybe I should be heavy-handed with the chia seeds more often! Well, if you don't mind, I'm going to do some meditation.'

I didn't mind. I didn't mind at all. Mum did meditation in her yoga studio (a shed with a carpet at the bottom of the garden) – it meant she would be out of the way and the coast would be clear. Although there was one thing I had to check.

'Is Dad out?'

'Yes,' she said, unpinning her apron. She lowered her voice. 'He's having some problems with a Trouble Client . . .'

'So you don't know when he'll be back?'

'I'm afraid not, but I don't think it will be

any time soon. Apparently he's been running all over town. I don't know how he does it,' she added softly, shaking her head.

As soon as Mum had gone into the garden, I grabbed the key from the bottom of the umbrella stand and called to Will, who still had his head in the front bushes. I opened the door to the study and pulled Will to the DADS machine. The tickertape from the machine was so long it was curling around lazily on the carpet below the shelf. The machine grunted and rolled out even further. It was a very busy day.

'What's that?' Will asked, genuinely curious.

'It's a list of people who need to . . . leave the Earth.'

'Do you mean space travel or do you mean abduction?'

'Neither.' I was getting tired of saying the

word but there was no way round it. 'I mean *death*. Bye-bye, game over, goodnight. You know, *death*.'

I walked over and pulled the tape through my fingers:

Mr Pete Hayes,
Ms Marjorie Davies,
Mrs Lucy Belfry,
Mr Humphrey Potter . . .

There she was. My hand shook as I tilted it for Will to see. **Mrs Sally Maggot.**

'Look.'

Will sauntered over, read it out loud and then slapped his hand over his mouth.

'You wrote that on there yourself!' he cried. But as he was talking, more names were being spat out of the machine, making the list curl and twist at our feet. 'Who's doing that?' he shrieked, showing signs of being a little freaked out.

And about time, really.

'It comes from the The Dead End Office. The place where they organise deaths. Look.' I pulled down the *Death Dictionary* from the shelf and opened it at *HEX*. 'I quote: "scheduled to die". And if the names get sent to the Direct Action Death System machine – this one – then it's for immediate action. It's all in here.' I tapped the book. 'Now we should go.'

Will's eyes bulged. He'd started to take notice of the books on Dad's shelves. *Natural Death Protocols*, he mouthed. Then he started whimpering.

'Can't you just tear her off?' he stammered.

'I can't. The tape is strong as steel,' I said, now speaking very fast so we could stop wasting time. 'Dad must have a special tool. And we really, really should go –'

'But Granny Maggot's on the list!' Will squealed, realisation dawning.

'I know. We need to get a move on. We have to get to her before Dad does.'

'Oh balaclavas! Jim, he's horrible!'

'He's a nice Death, actually,' I protested. 'But he is going to get Granny Maggot, if we don't stop him.'

Will rose up tall and puffed out his chest like a superhero. 'Over my dead body!'

That was the spirit. We were on our way! Almost.

When I opened Dad's study door, I spotted Hetty outside. She was wearing a wooden spatula tucked into her belt and a pair of ski goggles on her head which were so tight her eyebrows had been pulled halfway up her forehead. She was kicking her scooter, which was lying on the floor next to Dad's study door.

'Hetty, what are you doing?' I asked, pushing Will back in and shutting the door.

'Welcome to Scooter Mechanics Is Me,' she said.

'Don't you mean Scooter Mechanics Are Us?'

'Only if you play too. But if you're not playing it's just me. I can solve any scooter problem.

Workmanship guaranteed.' She kicked her scooter again.

'Why are you kicking it?'

'It's part of the mechanic's work,' she said. 'It's guaranteed.'

Like I said earlier, some things are really not worth arguing about. However, the location of Hetty's scooter mechanics business was giving me problems and I needed to kick her out of the way. Not literally, but I did need to get Will out of Dad's study without her seeing.

'Hetty, could you perhaps do that in the back garden?'

She looked at me, tutted and wiped her brow with the back of her hand. 'Not before you tell me why you were in Dad's study. You're not allowed in there, you know.'

'I know, but I was . . . looking for money.' I

knew she'd understand, what with all the money she steals for her 'horse fund'.

'Why?'

'I spent quite a lot at Streets and I owe the lady there lots of money for sweets.' It was true. I felt my heart beat a bit faster as I realised that this was something that needed solving sooner or later.

'How much?' Hetty asked. She was now making a show of wiping her oily mechanic's hands on her trousers.

'Twenty-five pounds.'

'Don't worry, I will sort it out for you, Jimble Wimble,' Hetty said. She ran into the kitchen and back out again a second later, waving a piece of paper. She pushed it against my chest and then wheeled her scooter out through the back door into the garden.

Give and Take. What was it this time?

Chapter 14

'Glad you're back,' said Kevin. 'The woman at number 62 has been giving me strange looks . . . He alright?' Kevin jutted his thumb at Will.

'He's fine!' I laughed, unconvincingly. 'But drive round the block again, will you?'

Will was far from alright. While I'd been talking to Hetty, Will had been watching the *DADS* tickertape spitting out names, and he'd kind of lost it. He'd gone pale and clammy, and all the 'over my dead body' stuff had vanished. In fact, he'd looked as if he might have been preparing himself to jump off a cliff or feed himself to the pigs. There was no sign of a superhero now, just a pale, slightly quaking boy.

Granny Maggot was dozing against a window and Fiona was occupied with editing her video, so I moved Will to the back of the bus where we wouldn't be heard. He walked stiffly, like he was made out of cardboard. I was worried he might be going into hibernation.

'Will, look at me,' I said. I grabbed his chin and turned his face towards mine. 'Will, look into my eyes. Tell me what you have just discovered.'

I shook his face. His cheeks wobbled.

'Your dad . . . is Death,' Will snivelled.

'Yes,' I nodded, glad that he'd grabbed the concept. 'Yes, that's right. But I'm not allowed to tell you. I'm not allowed to tell anyone!'

'We should tell Fiona?' he said, nodding to himself.

'Definitely not Fiona,' I said, quickly. Imagine how she'd react – she might think I was lying to get attention, or worse, she would hate me for being the son of the man who was Death and after her granny . . . She'd make my life hell. 'Will. Fiona mustn't know. She'd just make fun of us and waste time. She wouldn't believe it.'

'And if she did,' Will added, with eyes widening, 'she might kill your dad, which could create some sort of universal paradox . . .' Will straightened his back and his glasses. He might have snapped out of his trance, but his lip was still quivering as if it had a life of its own. 'We have to save Granny on our own, Jim,' he said. 'Just you and me.'

'Yes. And we will,' I said as calmly as I could. Calm is good for confidence.

'But how? You said it was her day to die!' Will said, starting to lose it again. 'If that evil machine said she's going to die today then how can we stop it? We can't stop the day from happening! Maybe we can't stop your dad, either. Maybe he's unstoppable, like an Ultimate Terminator Robot. Maybe he'll come along and . . . Aaargh!' Will shrieked, pointing at Granny Maggot. Her head had nodded forward and her eyes were closed.

'She's just asleep, Will,' I said. Granny Maggot shifted a little, and Will's shoulders relaxed. 'It's okay, she's safe.'

'Safe? *Safe?* Have you actually ever seen your dad doing deaths?' Will asked, sinisterly. I shook my head. 'Then how do you know he doesn't turn into an invisible vapour that can slip up nostrils and kill your brain while you're asleep?' His eyes were now moons. 'We have to wake her up! We need to keep her awake!'

Keeping Granny Maggot awake wasn't a bad idea. Not because Dad was an invisible vapour – I'm pretty sure vapours wouldn't bother with nifty trainers – but if Granny Maggot absolutely insisted on going home, Kevin and his 'just say the word' would make it impossible.

'I agree,' I said, patting Will's shoulder. 'We need to keep her awake. And if my calculations are correct, we only have to get through to midnight. If it's her "day",' – I made quote marks with my fingers to emphasise the importance of the word – 'then tomorrow she will be safe. That's only six hours away. See – it's going to be okay.'

There was a wheeze from Granny Maggot. We looked over at her. Her jaw dropped open and her dentures slipped from her top gums. Will scratched his chin.

'If you want to wake up a giant African land snail . . .' Will said, ignoring my impatient face, 'you have to give them a stimulating bath.'

'I don't fancy bathing your gran,' I muttered.

'Bath isn't the important word, Jim. The important word is *stimulating*. We have to keep Gran stimulated – she needs sounds, lights, things to do, things to keep her brain awake. Sitting on a bus is the worst thing. In a minute she'll be in deep sleep and then how will we stop the death vapour from creeping up her nose?'

I wanted to say that the death vapour theory was stupid but so long as Will was alert and producing biscuity bits of brilliance to keep

Granny Maggot alive, then he could believe whatever he wanted about Dad.

So far the biscuit had crunched in all the right places. If we could keep her brain functioning at all times, it would make moving her easier and make the approach of death a whole lot harder. And then, after midnight, it would all be over. Not *dead* over – but over as in there would be a new dawn, a new day, and a new schedule for Dad *without* Granny Maggot's name on it.

'I think the cinema would put her to sleep, so that's no good,' Will was saying. 'How about bowling? No, wait, Fiona hates bowling . . . Um, what about more cake. Battenberg, naturally –?'

'Will!' I said, seeing a poster on a lamppost outside. I pressed my face against the bus window. There were more posters, stuck everywhere, with bright neon writing and shouty lettering. 'Will! Where would we find lights, music, things to do, excitement, stimulation?'

'The West Midlands Snail-o-rama Museum? It has a carousel in the shape of a –'

'The fair, Will, the fair. Roberto's All-Night Funfair is in town!'

Will's mouth zipped into a smile.

'Yes! Jim, you're a genius! You've saved her!'

I blushed. 'I haven't saved her yet, Will. Even with all the fun of the fair, keeping Granny Maggot awake until midnight will be like trying to stop a chimpanzee stealing bananas from the fruit bowl.'

Will frowned. 'A genius wouldn't say that,' he said.

Chapter 15

Roberto's All-Night Funfair. It was a great idea.

But we had parents. And you can't just disappear for a whole evening without telling them where you're going. It doesn't work. Parents get worried, then cross, then twitchy. Parents can stop your pocket money. In my case, parents can delete your memory.

'What are we going to tell our parents?' I said. Will shrugged.

Then Fiona's phone rang. Her ringtone was a song by Imagine Dragons. She is so cool. Kevin chuckled and stopped the bus as if he knew what this was about. He turned and looked expectedly at Fiona as she answered it. She mumbled into the phone and it all sounded very serious. She finished the call and looked up at us and her green eyes were swimming as if she were going to cry, but her mouth was smiling, crookedly.

'That was Mum,' she said. 'She asked if Gran was still with us . . . She's talked to Dad and Dad's decided he wants to make up with Gran. We have to go back.'

Kevin chuckled again – and I knew he had something to do with it. Why Kevin had anything to do with us at all was baffling; it was almost like he was some huge speed-crazy guardian angel . . .

Fiona and Will hugged and cheered and Granny Maggot patted her hair in preparation.

'I've got an idea,' I announced, winking at Will. 'As a celebration, why don't we go to the fair afterwards? Roberto's All-Night Funfair is in town, and I've heard it's the best in the country.' There were nods and murmurs of approval.

'We should go all night long, until midnight,' said Will, which wasn't very subtle.

'Why don't you drop me back home, Kevin?' I suggested. 'I have to tell my parents anyway. Then you can pick me up again in . . .' I calculated the possibility of a long and annoying encounter with Hetty, 'half an hour. Then on to Roberto's.'

'Better than Battenberg!' Will shouted.

'Better than Battenberg!' said Mrs Maggot. I don't think she knew why she was saying it, but she was in a very good mood. Dicky was about to put the Lego behind him – and about time, too.

Kevin drove me home. Before I got off, Will came up to me.

'I'm putting these away now,' he said, taking off his glasses and tucking them in his jacket pocket.

'Why, Will? I thought the frames helped you focus?' Will had only recently started wearing glasses with no glass – just the frames – to help concentrate his mind and stop it from wandering off and thinking about other things.

'Sometimes you need to know what to focus on, don't you?' Will sighed. 'I've been so focused on being freaked out, when what I should be focusing on is the fact that you didn't have to tell me your dad was Death –'

'It's okay, Will,' I said.

'And you didn't have to spend the whole day with me –'

'Will, I like spending time with you –'

'And you didn't have to make deals with your sister to –'

'Oh, I nearly forgot,' I said, retrieving the contract from my pocket.

Give and Tak contact 2
Hetty will sort out Jim's munny problm
Jim will by Hetty fansie dressips
do it tudday

Oh, rats bums! Will took the contract from me and put his glasses back on.

'*Fansie dressips?* Is that a kind of cake? The name of a doll?'

'Fancy dress-ups . . .' I sighed. 'Just bits of

clothing so she can turn herself into Hetty the Homeless Witch or Hetty the Demon Street cleaner or Hetty of the Many Hats . . .'

'I've got many hats,' Kevin chortled. 'Every day another bloomin' hat.' He began rummaging around in a cupboard behind the driver's area and dragged out a box. 'I've had this lot for ages. You can have it if you like.'

I looked in the box – hats, scarves, gloves, glasses, jumpers . . .

'Wow, you've got a lot of disguises, Kevin,' Will wondered. 'Do you change to suit your environment. Like an octopus, perhaps, the most cunning of molluscs?'

'It's a box of lost property, porridge-brain,' Fiona winced, clearly embarrassed by her little brother.

'It's perfect, Kevin, thanks,' I said, stuffing it all into a plastic bag.

'*Myergh!*' came a shout from the back.

'Good luck with your dad,' I said, giving Will a quick hug. Then I turned to Kevin. 'Thanks for what you did with Dicky and Granny Maggot. It's really thoughtful.'

'I'm fully on board with your Random Acts of Kindness, Jim,' he smiled.

'Yes, so I see . . . Well, thank you. And could you pick me up in half an hour?'

'How could I say no to the Random Happiness Generator! Toot toot!'

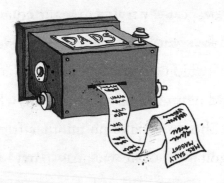

Chapter 16

Hetty was sitting at the top of the stairs.

'What have you got for me, Jim?' she said
with a touch of wickedness. I threw the bag
of lost property up the stairs and she
squealed with delight and ran into her room
with it.

Mum was just returning from the garden,
clutching her mobile phone.

'I didn't think you were supposed to make
phone calls while meditating, Mum,' I laughed.

I was desperately trying to make conversation while I thought up an excuse for going out all night. I couldn't involve Will, so what would I say? I'd never stayed overnight anywhere else before. Should I make up another friend? Say I was going to a late birthday party? Ask her to trust me?

'I know, I know,' Mum said. 'I was deep in the zone, too!' She shook the phone above her head with frustration. 'Sorry, Jim, I just got completely out of the zone there.'

'Are you alright, Mum?' I asked.

'Yes, yes. It's just, I was hoping to have a patchouli bubble bath and a relaxing evening on the sofa watching that new cooking show, but now I've got to go up north to meet a mung bean supplier. It's hours away – I'll have to stay overnight.'

Yes, you heard that right. Mung bean. Words

like mung bean are part of our everyday life. It's embarrassing.

'You're staying overnight just to get mung beans?'

'You'd be surprised how many of my customers like mung beans, Jim!' Mum declared. 'And this new chap says today is the only day we can do a deal – he's throwing in some alfalfa and broccoli sprouts for free. Isn't that marvellous?'

'Great . . .' I smiled. 'So does that mean Dad's home tonight?'

Mum shrugged. 'We don't know how long this *trouble* is going to go on for. So Indigo's going to come over and babysit overnight. I've made up the spare room for her. I hope she's here soon or I'll miss my train.'

Just then, Indigo swept through the open front door. Indigo is the daughter of Mum's yoga instructor. She's not very yoga-y, though. She's moody and spends most of her time on her phone talking to friends or taking photos of her nails.

Mum gave her some instructions (which Indigo didn't listen to, because she was looking at her phone), then kissed my cheek, snatched her bag and rushed out of the door.

'Hi Indigo,' I said.

Indigo didn't answer. She just loped into the living room and sat herself down on the sofa. Hetty and I don't like Indigo very much, and she doesn't like us; but that's just why, at that very moment, I loved her. Indigo was so rubbish at babysitting she never ever checked to see if we were okay, and that gave me the perfect opportunity to disappear for the evening. Although, there was the issue of Hetty.

I ran upstairs and knocked on Hetty's door. She answered, covered in material.

'Are you . . . a jumble sale?'

'No I am not!' she said, offended. 'I'm a Wardrobe Demon.'

'So you like the dress-ups, then?' I said, spotting several items on her person that had come from the bus – an umbrella, a rain hat and a Manchester United scarf.

'It's brilliant, Jim. See, I told you Give and Take was good. Everyone's a winner!' She waved her Manchester United scarf in the air, though I wasn't sure they were still top of the league.

'Hetty, I have a problem. I need you to cover for me.'

'Okay. I like this game. Let me just get a contract ready . . .' Hetty went to her drawers and pulled out a piece of paper.

'Now speak,' said Hetty, pen poised.

'I need to go out for the evening. All evening.'

'And I know why. You're going to Roberto's All-Night Funfair, aren't you? I saw the posters.'

'No . . .' I said. 'Fairs are so lame and childish.' I hoped it was convincing – I couldn't risk telling Hetty, in case she mentioned it to Dad . . .

'So you're meeting a girl, then,' she tried, waggling her eyebrows.

I was about to protest, but actually, it was quite a handy excuse. If she didn't manage to keep it a secret, at least no one would suspect I was with Will. I love Will, but I'm pretty sure when I start going on dates, I won't be taking him with me.

I winked.

'You *are* meeting a girl!' she cried with glee. 'Okay, then, but it will cost you. Big time! Let's see – out with a girl, gone all evening, lying to the babysitter, and to Mum and Dad . . . Hmmmm.'

Hetty scribbled out the new Give and Take Contract and pushed it against my chest.

'I will go downstairs and talk to Indigo and you can sneak out. If she asks where you are I'll say you've gone to bed because you're not feeling well. I will fill your bed with pillows, too. That's my side of the deal. Your side of the deal is written on that piece of paper – and you signed it, Jim. You signed it.'

It simply said:

By Hetty a big horsy
tudday

Chapter 17

Granny Maggot's reunion with Will's dad Dicky went well. Apparently they hugged without stopping through three Black Eyed Peas songs and then shared pizza. Will even demonstrated the pizza-eating as he recounted the story to me, which wasn't necessary because I know how to eat pizza.

'They hardly said a word to each other, Jim,' Will said. 'It was as if they were having a conversation without talking, like they could feel what they wanted to say. A bit like snails –'

Although I was glad Granny Maggot and Dicky had got over the whole thirty-year Lego war, I'd had a discussion about snail telepathy with Will once before and I didn't want to hear it again.

'So they're friends again?' I interrupted.

'Yup,' Will smiled and then lowered his voice. 'The telepathy was so strong, I thought we'd never be able to leave, but I got Fiona excited by the idea of filming Gran on a roller-coaster, and Dad said he needed a nap, anyway, and it didn't matter now, because they had all the time in the world to catch up.' He stopped for breath. 'What did you tell your mum?' he asked.

I told Will about mung beans and Indigo. And Hetty's new demands, which was weighing on my mind (as if saving Granny Maggot wasn't enough).

'Now she wants a horse! If I don't get her one, I'm toast! She'll tell Mum I was out for the entire night, and I'll be in such trouble. What am I going to do?'

Will put his arm around my shoulder. 'Did you know that snails piggyback each other to save slime and energy?' he said softly. I didn't answer. Snails had no place in my current agony. 'Jim. I'm going to piggyback you, to save your slime.'

I looked up. 'I don't have any slime.'

'Rest your slime – and let me worry about Hetty's horse.'

'I'm not sure if that would be a good idea,' I said, as nicely as I could. 'Things run a bit more smoothly when my *slime* is involved . . .' I tailed off, not knowing why I was getting involved in this conversation.

'Don't worry, Jim. My focus range is much

bigger now, so I can help you find a way out of this.' Will tried to look around him 360 degrees like a demented owl. I tried not to laugh. 'I'll think of something.'

I had no doubt Will would think of something. The trouble was, that *something* might be whether the melting time for cheese had any link to the moon's orbit. You never could tell.

'Here we are!' bellowed Kevin, swinging the bus into a parking space.

'We're here, Granny,' Will said sweetly.

'Where?' she said, propping herself upright.

'At the funfair,' Fiona said, holding Granny Maggot's hand. It looked as frail as an autumn leaf next to Fiona's.

'Dicky loved the funfair . . .' Granny Maggot sighed happily. 'But I'm feeling ever so tired, now.'

'I'm not surprised, it's been a big day –' Kevin started.

'But we have to celebrate!' Will interrupted. Let's do something exciting, Gran.'

I caught Fiona's eye and did a rollercoaster motion with one hand and pointed at Granny Maggot. She grinned. A granny on the fairground rides would make brilliant filming.

'It's either that or we can go back to Riverside and I can tell you all about my boring school and boyfriends,' Fiona joked, suddenly on our side. I might have blushed at that bit.

Granny Maggot was looking out of the window at the sign above the park entrance. It was red and gold and surrounded with light bulbs the size of grapefruits. There was a letter missing.

ROBERTO'S
ALL-NIGHT UNFAIR

Chapter 18

Granny Maggot seemed to be wowed by the light bulbs above her. Forgetting Stanley's wheelchair, she stepped off the bus into the warm glow.

'Marvellous!' she sighed, as she twirled around beneath them. 'Oh, it reminds me of the dance halls . . . I was hot to trot in those days,' she remembered dreamily. 'You wouldn't believe it now, but there were men who would queue around the block just for a spin around the dance floor with me. Men with proper manners, they were.'

Will and Fiona smirked and shrugged at each other.

'Good *heeverning*, ravishing Signora,' said a man in a black top hat and white coat, rippling his Rs like Italian people do. It must have been Roberto, himself.

'Good evening to you, sir,' said Granny Maggot with a flutter of her eyes, still reliving her memories.

'Are you rrrrr-olling up for the funfair?' he said, taking her hand and kissing it gently.

'We're ready to roll,' said Will. 'What do you recommend?'

'Well-a. For tha lay-dee,' he began, still clutching Granny Maggot's hand, 'I recommend the Twairling Teacops.'

That's the Twirling Teacups to you and me.

He led us there in person and all five of us squeezed into one tiny teacup. We were wedged in so tightly all our bottoms were touching and we couldn't move. The tiny teacups rotated

slowly around a central teapot in which the ride controller – a skinny man with a face like a rat – was also playing plinky-plonk tunes on a xylophone. It was my idea of hell, but Granny Maggot was smiling and waving like the Queen to the queue of bored mums and dads waiting to collect their kids and go home.

And it went on. And on. And around . . . and around. And on . . .

'They're not twirling, they're hardly moving at all!' Fiona complained.

I was squashed next to her and probably feeling less bored than I should be, considering we weren't going very fast.

'It's rather pleasant,' said Kevin. 'Sally Magic likes it, don't you, Sally? . . . Sally?'

We all looked at Granny Maggot. Her eyes were drooping, her jaw had gone slack and her dentures were chattering.

'No!' shrieked Will, whipping his head round. He made big scared eyes at me – fearful of deadly vapours. 'FASTER!' Will shouted at the man in the central teapot, and every little child's face in every teacup turned to look at him. Fiona picked up her phone quicker than a High Noon cowboy. Her brother was about to make a real fool of himself and she wasn't going to miss it.

'I'm recording!' she announced.

'FASTER!' said Will again.

Then a slow chant started. *Faster! Faster! Faster!* Kids so small they didn't even know what FASTER meant were shouting it. Kids who were just learning to talk were shouting FARTER. Other kids were just looking like they were going to throw up and couldn't say anything.

The onlookers were laughing and the rat-faced fairground man in the see-through teapot in the middle of the ride shrugged and pushed his lever as far forward as it would go. The teacups accelerated, turning faster and faster until they were spinning madly. Granny Maggot woke up and Will cheered. Kevin chuckled. Kids vomited. Fiona was getting some excellent footage to put on the internet. It was 'video gold', she said.

When the ride eventually stopped to the sound of wailing children, everyone staggered dizzily off the teacups and it took some time for all of us to band together again. Every time one of us tried to reach another, our legs would suddenly whip us round so we were walking in a different direction.

'Will!' I said, grabbing on to his arm before the ground moved again.

'Right, what's next?' Will said, eagerly, checking his watch and falling sideways. 'We've got four hours to kill.'

'I could kill a burger!' Fiona exclaimed, crashing into us on wobbly legs.

'I could murder a cup of tea,' said Granny Maggot, crawling towards us on her hands and knees.

'I could slaughter a hot dog,' said Kevin, swaying dangerously.

Sitting on plastic chairs next to the Ring Of Fire attraction, under a picture of nearly naked people wrestling, we caught our breath and had some refreshments. I found myself sitting next to Kevin, who was eating a foot-long hot dog as daintily as a duchess at a tea party (if duchesses ever eat foot-long hot dogs). Between bites, he chuckled, and I wondered why this giant of a man we had never met before had spent the day with us. I'd never really thought about it – I was just happy that we had a chauffeur and a get-away vehicle. But really – what was he doing here with us?

Kevin slid his eyes sideways to meet mine, as if he'd read my thoughts.

'My mum died, you know,' he said, patting his mouth with a paper napkin. 'She got run over by a bus.'

'That's terrible! Not your bus?' I gasped.

'No. I was a train driver at the time. But it's why I swapped to buses. Trains pretty much drive themselves, but roads are like the Wild West with their crossroads, traffic lights, cars, pedestrians . . . I wanted to be sure that on my route, no life would ever be lost again. And I keep my eye out for vulnerable old ladies. I consider myself to be the Sherriff of the Streets.'

Kevin straightened his back and smiled at me,

as if he'd successfully answered any questions I might have.

'Kevin, I'm so sorry to hear about your mum. And I think being the Sherriff of the Streets is a brilliant job . . . But why have you spent the whole day with us?'

'Because of Sally Magic's special day out. It's important.'

'But I lied about the doctor's diagnosis. We were just trying to get on your bus.'

'You lied, but then again, you didn't lie,' he said, nodding wisely and pinning me with an intense look. He breathed in deeply. 'Because you never know when the last day is, do you?' He pinned me again. 'Did you ever think that today might actually *be* Sally's last day out?'

I gulped. He continued.

'You never know when it's going to happen, so my motto is *Carpe diem*. It's Latin. It means "seize the day". Which basically means *do it now*.'

'Do *what* now?'

'Everything. What you want. Just do it. Never occurred to me Mum would go under the 320 from Kings Cross to Barking, but if I'd known . . . Never got the chance. Never got the chance . . .' Kevin took another nibble of his hot dog.

'But helping us won't bring your mum back.'

'Your friend's granny reminds me of my mum, in lots of ways. My mum used to say "blergh", which isn't so different, and she smelt of lavender, and she loved Wotsits, so she did . . . I might be the Sherriff of the Streets, but I wear other hats, you know. I'm a do-gooder – I like to pay things forward, I like to do nice things for people just because I can, and I want to stop people from making the same mistakes I

did. One of my biggest mistakes was not doing good things for my mum when I could.'

So I had got to the bottom of Kevin's good deeds. And I was about to hug him, just for being the Sherriff of Impossibly Nice, but Will nudged me and pointed at Granny Maggot. Her eyes were open, but she was tilting sideways as if one side of her chair was sinking into the ground beneath. While we were scoffing burgers and hot dogs, and having heart-to-heart talks with Kevin the bus driver, Granny Maggot had been sipping her longed-for cup of tea, and was flooded with sleepiness.

'Wake up, Gran!' Will said loudly, taking her wrist.

'Always have a cup of tea before bed,' she said, drowsily.

'Not bed yet, Granny Maggot!' I said. 'Let's make the most of the fair! Plenty more to do.'

I looked around to see what we could do next, and that's when I saw a figure in the distance. It was tall, wearing dark clothing. It could have been anyone – anyone who liked dressing in black . . . But then it turned around in circles, searching. *It was Dad*. My heart thumped. No time to lose – we needed to get moving. Somewhere. Anywhere. Preferably a place where crowds of people would hide us.

And there was a queue outside the candyfloss tent.

Chapter 19

The air inside the tent was thick with sugary sweetness. Kids' eyes bulged as the candyfloss girl spun the pink wisps around sticks, again and again, until they looked like bulging candy caveman clubs. When we reached the front of the queue, Granny Maggot hesitated.

'This isn't like that popping stuff, is it? *Myergh!*'

'No, Gran, ' laughed Will. 'It's like clouds of sugar. You'll love it.'

Will looked at me and nodded wisely. A trip to Streets the Newsagent had taught us what sugary things did to Granny Maggot. This would definitely keep her awake – and if she did go nuts like a chimpanzee, the funfair was the right place to do it.

Will got her the most enormous candyfloss which obscured her entire face and gave me a good idea. If I had a disguise – if I could be obscured – then I could keep an eye on Dad without being seen. Besides, being covered head to toe in candyfloss would please Fiona, because I'd look like an idiot, which is exactly what she likes.

I asked the candyfloss girl to create my disguise.

'You mean,' she said, chewing slowly on gum, 'you want to be the stick?'

'Yes,' I said, hurriedly. 'I want to be the stick.'

'You do realise it will be sticky, right?' The girl wrinkled her nose.

'Yes, yes, I know that. I'll be a sticky stick.'

'Weird . . .'

Glad that we'd got to the end of that conversation, I handed over a handful of money, and the girl spun me round and round, twisting me in wisps of sugar until I was a giant pink walking cloud. People took photos. Will poked me two eye holes, Granny Maggot said I was 'mad as cottonwool', and Kevin had to be stopped from picking pieces off me and eating them. It isn't as nice as it sounds, being covered in candyfloss. It's sticky and scratchy. But Fiona loved it so much she was grinning, with full dimples, and at least I now had a disguise.

As soon as we stepped out of the tent, people started pointing. I was being noticed, but at least I wasn't being recognised and I could relax a little. But Granny Maggot had begun dozing against a tent pole, gripping her untouched candyfloss to her chest, like a teddy bear. I quickly broke off a piece and stuffed it into her mouth and she woke from the electric buzz that comes from 100% sugar and 20% E-number.

'That is the funniest thing ever, Jim. A giant candyfloss feeding people candyfloss. Awesomely random. I'm impressed,' said Fiona.

I went bright red. Luckily she couldn't see, because I was already bright pink.

'Come on, everyone, there's room on the Dodgems,' I said.

'I think we'd better call them Bumper Cars,' said Will. 'More likely to keep her awake.'

I glanced around me – at the spinning rides and ice-cream stalls, at the swinging boats and duck fishing games. And then, on top of the

Helter Skelter, I saw his silhouette. I could tell it was Dad by the way he was scratching his head, like he does when he's faced with maths. But although he was recognisable, right now he was Death, and I felt real fear.

Of course, we could go on the run again, but where to? Roberto's All-Night Funfair seemed as good a place to hide as anywhere. Nowhere was easier for a hider and harder for the hunter than the fair. It was huge, branching out in all directions, from the food stalls at the edges to the carriages of screaming kids on the arms of terrifying rides, high up in the sky. It was also getting dark, and although light bulbs were blazing above every attraction, on the ground the crowds milled around in the gloom, providing easy camouflage. So long as I could see Dad, and I could see that he couldn't see me, then we'd be okay.

Over the next few hours it went brilliantly. We dodged Dad while getting the most out of our trip.

We did the Bumper Cars, where Kevin's rally-fever made eight small children and three grown adults cry (he felt terrible about it afterwards). We did the Rifle Range, where Granny Maggot won a box of jelly babies and we all agreed Will should never, ever, ever be allowed to hold a weapon. Then we all went to the First Aid Tent with Kevin while he got the rifle cork that Will had fired removed from up his nostril. Then we had a small incident with some stray dogs and my candyfloss costume until Fiona coaxed them away with Granny Maggot's jelly babies. Then Granny Maggot had a granny-fit about the dogs eating her jelly babies so we went back to the Rifle Range and discovered that like her granny,

Fiona also had a really good aim (I knew she would). She won *six* boxes of jelly babies (and didn't share any of them except with Granny Maggot). And then we played follow my leader in a conga chain, me at the front, weaving away from Dad whenever I saw him. After that, we did the Octopus, which was one of those terrifying high up ones which spun round and round. Will was so scared he tried to get into the foetus position.

It was quarter to midnight when we all stumbled off the Octopus feeling as if we'd been in a boxing ring with The Incredible Hulk. Fiona was white with fear, Will was sick in some bushes, Kevin got stuck in the narrow exit gates and I was pretty sure my kneecap was cracked.

And Granny Maggot? Granny was gone.

Oh no . . . Granny gone? The pain left my

kneecap and shot straight to my head as panic
set in. I grabbed Will's arm.

'C-c-can you see Granny Maggot anywhere?'
I stuttered. He boggle-eyed me back.

'Where is she?' Will yelled. 'I thought she was
on the ride with Kevin!'

'She couldn't fit in my carriage,' said Kevin,
blushing. 'So they were putting her on the next
one.'

'Oh great,' Fiona tutted. 'She was probably
scared out of her wits and wandered off
confused.'

'She could be anywhere,' said Kevin, which
wasn't helpful.

'Right – we need to split up,' said Fiona.
'North, south, east and west. Go!' She was *so*
forceful . . .

They went looking for Granny Maggot but I
went looking for Dad. When I went on the

Octopus, I'd seen him standing by the Twirling Teacups. But he wasn't there now. I had a horrible thought that Granny Maggot had gone back there in search of the man with good manners. I needed to find him – or her – before something went very wrong. But the night crowds, which were mostly long-legged teenage boys, were making things impossible. Although a few stopped in amazement to let through a kid dressed in candyfloss, most shuffled along at a slow pace, blocking my view. The only way was to get up high and find a lookout point. One that didn't go round and round and make you sick. Of course – the Helter Skelter. It was the perfect lookout point. That's why Dad had been there.

Climbing to the top of a Helter Skelter in head-to-toe candyfloss is at least eight times as tricky as doing it without. I could tell by the amount of sweat trickling down my face, which had instantly mixed with the candyfloss to create pink sticky rivers. I licked away what I could from my cheeks and looked out over the fair.

Below me swarms of people were waiting their turn for rides. If Mrs Maggot had gone looking for Roberto, he shouldn't be that hard to spot. I searched for a top hat. I did find Roberto, eventually, but it didn't look as if he was in entertaining mode any more – he was behind one of the caravans swigging wine from a bottle. I eventually spotted Kevin, Will and Fiona; they were at the Rifle Range again, and I have to admit I felt a bit let down. Especially by Will, who knew that this wasn't a family trip to the fair but a death-defying challenge – did he expect me to do it all on my own?!

I looked back at the Teacups, which was now spilling out its dizzy riders, and Granny Maggot wasn't among them. Nothing was to be seen of her, or Dad. Put nothing and nothing together and what do you get? Even Dad could work that one out. My heart sank.

I was about to rip off my candyfloss coating in an I've-given-up kind of way when I saw a small hunched figure making its way to the bottom of the field, where taxis were lining up to take fair-goers home. Someone behind me shouted, 'Get a move on, you puffball,' and I was shoved. I didn't even have a mat, so I spiralled down the Helter Skelter on my backside, sparking an increasingly intense smell of burning sugar. As I tore down one of the spirals I saw Roberto look up in alarm (as you would, if you saw a giant candyfloss) and run towards the Helter Skelter.

I landed, shredded and sweet-smelling, on the mats at the bottom of the ride.

'Smoke!' slurred Roberto, as he helped me up off the floor. He now had splats of red wine down his crisp white costume. 'There's smoke coming from your bum!' he added, in a not very Italian accent, and started slapping at the burning candyfloss embers on my backside. We were interrupted by a man so big that the tattoo-ed anchors on his arms were life-size.

'Mr Roberto,' he rasped.

'It's out!' said Roberto, dusting his hands. 'Remind me to put up a sign later – No Candyfloss on the Helter Skelter . . . Now, what is it, Pepe?' He said it like *Peppay*.

'We got a call out,' said Pepe.

'A call out? But we shut the fair in five minutes. Can't they wait?'

'It can't wait, Rob. An old lady is lost. She's poorly. She needs to be found.'

Good thinking! I thought. And I was fleetingly proud of my team.

'Oh, very well,' sighed Roberto, swigging from a new bottle that had appeared in his hand. 'Pass me the tannoy.'

Enormous Pepe passed him a speaker phone.

'Here you are, Rob. The man asked if you can make the message to a Granny Sally Maggot – tell her there's a lift waiting, and to meet him at the big wheel.'

The man? That wasn't Fiona, Will and Kevin the bus driver, which added up to three (and I did that without a calculator). It was Dad. That meant death was still around. That meant . . . I couldn't take off my candyfloss disguise. I could have cried.

'Laydeeees and Giant-el-men,' said Roberto,

breaking into his fake Italian accent. 'This is a messitch for Grainy Saily May-got. Grainy Saily May-got – your lift is a-waiting-a. Come to the big wheel-a. Come to the big wheel-a, stray away!'

'Your Italian accent is great,' I gasped.

'I know,' said Roberto, before stumbling forward for an unexpected roll in the grass. Wine will do that to you, I'm told.

I didn't have time to worry about Roberto's drunkenness and weird accents or Pepe's outrageously large anchored biceps. I needed to get to the Big Wheel fast.

It was time to put on a Formula Onesie. I repeat: time to put on a Formula Onesie.

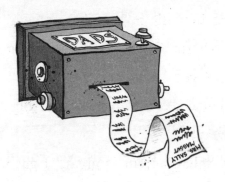

Chapter 20

I got to the Big Wheel at the same time as the others, including Granny Maggot, who was so tired she was bent over double, her hands nearly trailing on the ground.

'Jim!' Will shouted. 'Did you hear what the big voice in the sky said?'

'Yes,' I said, endlessly amazed at Will's brain processing. 'But we only have two minutes until midnight. We're going to make it.'

'But he'll be here any second,' Will cried. 'He'll get her at the eleventh hour!'

'Well, the eleventh hour and fifty-ninth minute,' said Kevin, overhearing the last bit. 'I'm good at timetables, see. What's the rush?'

'Oh, um,' Will froze. His eyes rolled around his head as he tried to think.

'Last ride's at midnight, and for my Random Acts of Randomness project the Big Wheel is absolutely a must. Old lady on a Big Wheel? It's got to be done.'

'What you on about?' Fiona interrupted.

'And . . . and . . .' I said, as if I knew what I was about to say. 'And . . . Granny Maggot, have you ever been on the Big Wheel before?'

'No. No . . .' Mrs Maggot said, yawning.

We looked up at the Big Wheel, with its little dangly carriages swaying in the breeze.

'Then *Carpe diem*,' I cried. '*Carpe diem!*'

Kevin went a bit misty-eyed and patted me on the shoulder.

'Oh, for heaven's sake,' Fiona butted in. 'This is stupid.'

'Why? Are you scared of heights or something, Fiona?' It was a brave thing to say, but I knew it would work.

'Me? Afraid of heights? Not likely. Come on, Granny. Come on, Will. Get in line! We're going up!'

We all got in line and the carriages were filling up fast, until there was just one left . . . One left for us.

'We can't all go!' I whispered to Will. 'It only takes three. Kevin would need a whole one to himself and my costume might fly off. Go Fiona, go Will, go Granny Maggot. Go!'

Fiona stopped and looked at me with a bit of a weird expression. I thought she was working a jelly baby out of her teeth with her tongue, but she wasn't. It was a smile with a hint of something very un-Viking-like – friendliness. She handed me a ticket.

'Something I won at the firing range. Will asked me to give it to you. Seems only fair after everything that's happened today. You've been truly random, Jim Wimple.'

'What is it?' I asked, taking the ticket.

'It's waiting for you at the big toy firing range, okay?'

Then the three Maggots jumped into the carriage and the safety bar was fixed over their lap. I stepped back quickly and the ride assistant raised his hand to the controller. They were nearly on their way . . . We had done it. We had cheated death, dodged the schedule, proved that the Human Existence machine and *DADS* could be beaten. In one minute – just sixty seconds – Granny Maggot's day to die would be over.

'Stop the ride!' a voice I knew called out.

Dad was standing right next to me. He wasn't alone. He was with a woman wearing a black cloak. I looked down – *nifty trainers*! Her hands were on her hips. She was poised for action. Dad turned to look at me. From the corner of my eye I could see his expression through a candyfloss filter. It was calm, but intense. I pulled the remaining folds of candyfloss closer over my face and shrunk back into the crowd a little. My heart was thumping. But if he'd seen me he'd have said something, wouldn't he? *Phew*. That was close!

'What is it, mate?' said the ride assistant. 'We shut after this ride. Can't it wait?'

'The elderly lady can't go on,' Dad said firmly.

'Oh, right,' said the ride assistant. 'Why's that?'

'She's ill.'

'Oh, right,' said the ride assistant again. 'Sorry love, you'd better get off.'

'Who are you?' Fiona sneered. The bright lights of the Big Wheel were in their eyes and they couldn't make out Dad's face. But Will knew who it was. He looked like a hare caught in the headlights.

'I'm from the care home,' said Dad.

Fiona squinted, trying to make out his features. Will's cheeks bulged. I wondered if he had gas. Something was brewing.

'Look,' droned the ride assistant, unamused. 'We don't have time for this. Get off, lady.'

'NOOOOoooooooo,' said Will, his voice erupting like I'd never heard before. Not even when I asked if I could take apart his Lego model of Big Ben so I could use the beige-colour bricks for my Lego safari camp. 'NOOOOooooo,' he boomed. 'Because . . .'

Please don't tell them my Dad is Death, I prayed. *Or he'll know I told you! Please don't say it. Focus, Will* (but he wasn't wearing his glasses).

Will looked odd, as if he was constipated or something. Would his brain work? Had his brain slime dried up? I squeezed my eyes tight, knowing that was dangerous because of the candyfloss. I might never open them again . . .

'My granny is ill . . .' he began, with a voice of authority.

'No I'm not. I'm not ill –' Granny Maggot started to say, confused, but Fiona hushed her with a jelly baby. She wanted to hear what her brother was so bold about.

' . . . but she said she wants to go on the Big

Wheel if it's the last thing she ever does. It's her last wish. So the granny rides!'

'Yeah. The granny rides,' I called out in a muffled voice, hoping that people would join in, just like they did on the Twirling Teacups. It didn't take long. One or two at first, then more and more.

The granny rides, the granny rides, the granny rides, the crowds started chanting.

Kevin, full of *Carpe diem*, shouted, 'I can't hear you!' and flapped his arms like a dragon trying to take off. It energised the crowd and they began to say it louder and louder and louder, until everyone in the funfair was chanting: *the granny rides, the granny rides, the granny rides*!

The ride assistant stared at my dad.

'Looks like the granny rides,' he said, smirking, and did a thumbs-up to the controller.

The controller took the cue and set the wheel in motion to the sound of cheering and clapping and screams of delight from everyone – everyone apart from me, because my lips had stuck together. As the carriages creaked their way up and around the wheel, people were crying and laughing as if they'd just watched a litter of kittens being rescued by a hunky fireman. I tried not to cry in case my eyes glued together, too. I saw Will's triumphant face and I inwardly cheered as I saw Granny Maggot, Fiona and Will climbing higher. They were up! They were up, moving high above the chanting crowd, moving away from Dad and The Woman who were standing underneath, and, if I was right – if my theory was right – moving towards another day of life. With only twenty seconds to go!

Fiona, Will and Granny Maggot had smiles

big as bananas. And as they neared the top I heard Granny Maggot safe and sound, screaming: 'This is best time of my whole life! I love it! I love it! I love it! Yipeeee!'

Then I saw The Woman, quick as liquid, jump onto the central frame of the Big Wheel. And suddenly I realised who she was. She must be from the Misadventures department of The Dead End Office – an expert in taking lives in sticky situations. Dad must have called for back-up to help him get rid of his Trouble Client. Although she wasn't trouble yet, was she? It was still her day to die. She was still officially no trouble at all. I didn't understand . . .

The Woman pulled herself up – and it wasn't hard if you weren't afraid of heights, because the Big Wheel is a structure of ladders and bars. Up and up she went, up the centre and right to the top, where she waited. And she wouldn't have to wait long. Her coat flapped in the high-up breeze. I saw her arm extend. I strained to see what she was doing, but she was a dark silhouette against a dark sky and the details were lost. But I could see Granny Maggot's carriage climbing higher, towards the very top.

With ten seconds to go . . .

By now people had started freaking out a bit. Who was that woman? What was she doing? I saw Roberto look at his bottle of wine and shake his head.

'Yipeeee!' squealed Granny Maggot, rocking the carriage dangerously. 'I can see everything from here!'

I could see Fiona and Will both had their arms around her.

They reached the top.

'I feel like I'm flying,' Granny Maggot called. 'I'm flying!'

Just one second to go . . .

I saw a flash of white as The Woman reached forward.

The carriage descended.

Granny Maggot's sleeping face was serene and happy, as if she'd just breathed in the scent of a rose garden in paradise. And it was still. Very still. I'd failed Granny Maggot – death had caught up with her.

Will and Fiona were either side of her, looking dazed. I knew that look. I'd seen it on Will before. She – The Woman – had erased their memories. I felt panic build inside me, unstoppable, like a volcano.

I had to get away. I had to get out of there fast before Dad and The Woman wiped the memories of everyone there. Including me.

Will and Fiona were still sitting in the carriage, mouths hanging open, blinking. They knew nothing of today's adventure, and there was nothing I could do about it. I had to get out of there.

I fled, trailing candyfloss, away from the Big Wheel and past the Twirling Teacups, away from Roberto and Pepe, away from the fair. But not before I checked in at the big toy firing range. If Fiona had won me something then I wasn't about to forget it. I handed in the ticket and grabbed my prize and ran.

The prize was a horse, of course. A giant cuddly horse. They'd won it while I was at the Helter Skelter. What did I tell you? *Biscuity brilliance!*

Chapter 21

Will called me first thing in the morning. I was so tired that when he told me his gran had died in the night I almost cried. Will did cry – big heaving hiccups – and I knew I had to go over and be with him at this terrible time. It's what a best friend would do; plus, I have to admit that, as my brain kicked into gear, I grew curious about what, if anything, Will remembered about the day we tried to save Granny Maggot. I shot off on my scooter, before I had to face any questions from Indigo (who I imagined wasn't a very good morning person), Hetty (still whistle-snoring in her room) or Dad (who I hoped and prayed was asleep in his).

Will's mum answered the door and I followed her into the kitchen. She flicked on the kettle and turned to me. Her eyes were smiley and sad at the same time. She wasn't dancing.

'Sorry, Jim Wimple, love,' she said. 'I'm all over the place today. Just had a call – my sister's had a little girl. Desperate for a kid, she was. It's wonderful news. Will's got a new cousin.' She burst into tears. 'And I suppose you've heard about . . .?'

'Yes,' I said. 'I'm sorry about Will's gran.'

'Yeah, well . . . At least we got to see her just before she went. And at least she and Dicky made up. Imagine if they hadn't . . .' She nodded her head towards Will's dad, who was curled up in an armchair in the corner of the kitchen. He was a huge man, but he suddenly seemed very small. 'Anyway, I know Will would love to see you, so go on up.'

Will was sitting on his bed, still in his pyjamas. He was carrying Maximus, like an ordinary kid would carry a pet kitten, in the crook of his elbow.

'I'm not putting on my glasses today,' he said. 'Or my clothes.'

'No.' I sat by his side and stroked Maximus's shell. It just seemed the right thing to do. 'How do you feel?' I asked.

He sniffed and shrugged. 'I loved her.'

'I know,' I said. And I didn't know what else to say.

'We had a great day, though, didn't we?'

We had a great day? How much could he remember?

'Which was your favourite bit?' I asked, carefully.

'I think it was when we were feeding the ducks . . .' Will placed a kiss on Maximus, as if he was reliving the tenderness. *So he definitely remembers everything up to the ducks . . .*

'And what about dancing with your mum?'

'Granny loved that,' he murmured. *He remembers coming back here for the disco, too . . .*

'And the Teacups?'

'Oh yeah. That was mad.'

He remembers the start of the fair as well! I wondered how far I should push it.

'And the Rifle Range – remember how good she was at winning jelly babies?'

'I know!' Will sniffed a little laugh. He let out a huge sigh. 'I can't believe she stayed as late as eleven o'clock!' Will shook his head. 'She's normally asleep by eight.'

He couldn't remember the Big Wheel, then. Not the final moments. Dad had taken an hour, He'd changed Will's memory from eleven p.m. onwards. Why not the whole day? Will suddenly gasped and unwittingly tightened his grip on Maximus.

'Oh bloomin' bowler hats, Jim! It's probably what killed her, isn't it! I hadn't thought of that . . . We did too much with her! Maybe she couldn't take the excitement. Maybe she –'

'She had the time of her life, Will,' I said calmly and firmly, taking his pet snail and returning it to its tank for safety. I sat back down and put my arm around him. 'Remember the first time she swung round Kevin's double-decker bus – how much fun did she have? And she made a new friend, made up with your dad, had a "food adventure", played with ducks and pigeons . . . She rediscovered her love of life. And most importantly, she rediscovered her love for you.' I felt mushy saying that, but Will nodded furiously, tears (or maybe snot) dripping onto his lap. 'I bet if she could have chosen how to spend her very last day, that would have been it exactly. And how many people get to say that, eh?'

'I suppose so, Jim. Thank you. Did Mum tell you about our new baby cousin?'

'She did, Will. It's brilliant news.'

'I think they're going to call her Sally.' Will looked up and smiled. I felt a hot tear spring from nowhere and roll down my cheek.

A noise came from Fiona's room. It was one of those sounds – could be laughter, could be crying – so Will and I went to check on her. Turned out it was both. Fiona was lying on her front on the floor, her face slippery with tears, looking at her phone. She stroked the hair off her face when she saw us, and patted the carpet next to her.

'Come and have a look,' she hiccupped. 'It's our day with Granny.'

Will and I lay down either side of Fiona and the three of us peered at the little screen with its shaky film of three kids, a grown-up and a granny. Every now and then we laughed so hard our stomachs ached and we had to curl up on the floor.

'I love this bit!' Fiona sniffed, pointing at me covered in candyfloss. She nudged me. 'King of Random, that's what you'll be called from now on.'

What I'll be called? By whom? Oh no, Fiona was obviously planning to upload these videos to her channel . . .

'Are you putting these on the internet?' I asked, nervously.

Fiona looked at me with her green cat-eyes and smiled a lop-sided smile. 'Nah. Although I'm sure the entire universe would love to see you as a giant candyfloss, this is about our last day with Granny. It's personal. It wouldn't be right.'

'Our last day . . .' Will wailed, remembering.

As for me, I was relieved. No internet. *Phew!* If Dad saw Fiona's videos he'd know what I'd been up to, and exactly why he'd had so much trouble doing his job yesterday. 'So who'll be calling me King of Random, then?'

'Me,' Fiona said, warmly. 'Just me.' As she turned back to the film, I felt a little buzz of happiness.

We went backwards and forwards through the video to various times of the day, laughing at Kevin's rally driver face, Will's mad Teacup chant, my over-the-top rant at the duck pond (which I had to blame on an Unexpected Random Act of Randomness) . . . Then the phone battery ran out. Just at the bit where Granny had won a box of jelly babies; the last image we saw was her face, unfolded from a wrinkled bag of concentration to a wide smile of pure happiness.

We all rolled onto our backs and stared at the ceiling. There was a thoughtful silence.

'You want to know something weird?' Will sniffed. 'They said when they found Granny she had the biggest smile on her face. Makes me think that death might not be that horrible.'

Chapter 22

I already knew that Death wasn't horrible. My dad was one of the nicest, kindest and happiest people you could ever meet. But right now, he wasn't very happy. And I didn't know why.

It was the day after our adventures with Granny Maggot, and with her gone everything should have returned to normal. But Dad sat through a whole episode of *Mr Bean* without slapping his thigh once. He seemed anxious. Mum made him an Uplifting Wind (banana and wild fern smoothie) and waved her arms above his head with something she called 'Healing Mantras'; Hetty said he could have a go on her new giant cuddly horse for free; and I even asked him to do The Cold Eye, thinking it might stir up some feelings, but nothing worked. Dad was glum.

And then the phone rang. He sat bolt upright and I saw sweat pop out on his nose. This was no ordinary call. This was a call from The Dead End Office. I knew in an instant that this was what Dad had been dreading. I'd already been nosy (and sneaky), much nosier and sneakier than I'd ever been, but I had to be nosy again now. I needed to find out whether Dad's boss was going to make life better or worse for the Wimple-Reapers.

Dad took the call in his study, so I crept upstairs and picked up the other phone. I carefully put it to my ear, and held my breath. The conversation between my dad and The Dead End Office had already started.

'. . . *total disgrace,*' growled the voice on the phone. It was Dad's boss.

'I know, I know, Mr Sinister. It won't happen again,' mumbled Dad, ever so meekly.

'Just because Mrs Black was in the area doesn't mean you can call her in to help with your workload,' said the voice.

'I know. I'm very grateful to her.'

'Next time you fail to stick to schedule, it has to be lodged as a Trouble Client, and plans have to be made accordingly. You jumped the gun, Grim. Misadventures is overworked as it is, especially at weekends.'

'I understand,' said Dad. 'Will there be . . . consequences?'

There was a long pause. Mr Sinister was

making Dad squirm, which made me so ashamed and so angry I had to stop myself from shouting **STINK FACE** down the phone.

'No. Not this time. Not this time, Grim.'

I whooshed a sigh of relief then quickly put the phone down and crept down the hall to my bedroom.

At dinner that night, Dad apologised for having been so glum and even did some *Mr Bean* impressions to show he was feeling better. He swapped his cutlery round so he was holding his potato still with a knife and cutting it with a fork. Hilarious. He thought so, anyway, and that's all that mattered.

'My Uplifting Wind sorted you out,' Mum said. She pointed her fork at him. 'I knew it would. You should trust the power of nature more. And try to get a more even work-life balance.'

'I'll show you how to balance, Dad,' said Hetty, oblivious to what was really going on. 'But it will cost you.'

'Why will it cost him?' I laughed.

'Give and take, Jim. You know about that.'

'Of course, Hetty,' I smirked. 'It's a two-way thing.'

'Speaking of two-way things,' Dad said, looking at me with his Intense Look, which is like The Cold Eye's sweeter little sister, 'did you happen to be anywhere near the upstairs phone earlier today?'

The Intense Look – which is like a dagger wrapped in pretty ribbon – would make any good boy shake violently and spill the beans on the spot. And I was scared that I would – that I'd tell him I'd listened to his conversation and heard all about the Granny Maggot episode and then he'd memory-wipe me and it would all be over . . . But I was no longer a good boy, it seemed, because I smiled with the face of an angel and said:

'No. Why?'

Dad looked at me a little while longer to be sure.

'Nothing.' He shook his head. 'Nothing at all. Don't worry about it . . . Oh, there is one more thing. Did you visit the all-night funfair when it was in town?'

I gulped. 'No. Why?'

'I thought maybe you might have gone with some friends.'

'You do look tired, Jim,' Mum said, looking concerned. 'There's some Uplifting Wind left –'

'No,' I said carefully, trying to control my voice. 'I didn't go to the all-night funfair.'

'No, he definitely didn't,' Hetty said, winking at me. 'He was horsing around with me!'

'And how's that friend of yours – William Maggot?'

'He's okay. Well, no, he's a bit sad, actually. He called this morning. His granny died.'

'Ah. Well, give him our deepest sympathies, won't you?' said Dad. 'Which reminds me, I have to pop out quite soon.'

'Got time for some treacle pudding?' Mum asked.

'Treacle pudding? That's not very Zing Zong Zen, is it?' laughed Dad.

'The treacle's made from the sap of the baobab tree, actually,' said Mum. 'Supposed to aid well-being of the pancreas.'

'Right,' said Dad, and gave me a wink. 'I might liver to regret this . . . Get it? Pancreas, Liver . . .'

The jokes were back, and so was Dad.

Chapter 23

Hetty crept into my room that night just before bed. She often comes for a snuggle; even if she's spent the day being Hetty Warrior or Hetty the Brother Hater, she'll turn up, Bo-Bo under her arm, for a cuddle at the end of the day. She slipped into bed alongside me and began to talk, even though she had her thumb in her mouth.

'Jimble?'

'Yes, Hetty.'

'You know the Give and Take thing?'

'What now, Hetty? I gave you a horse. You can't want anything else from me.'

'I don't!' she said, crossly, with a furrowed brow. She pulled out Bo-Bo and stuck her hand into his stuffing through one of his many holes.

'I forgot to give you this,' she said, bringing out a little bag.

I sat up and opened it. Twenty-five pounds!

'But, Hetty . . . How?'

'Sunny Rise, Super Green and Forest Fresh.'

'Those are names of Mum's smoothies.'

'Or Mum's homemade famous face-packs, used by people like the Prime Minister's wife and Sharon Osborne . . . *Apparently*. That's what I told Indigo. I sold them to her. Ten pounds each or three for twenty-five.'

'Hetty, you little rascal!' I was shocked, but I supposed I shouldn't have been. Hetty is Hetty – i.e. Utterly Brilliant. She giggled and tickled me in the ribs until I begged her to stop.

'So we're even.'

'Yes, Hetty, we are,' I smiled. 'And thank you.'

'No problem, wee wee face,' she said, and slipped out of my room and into her own.

When Hetty had gone, I lay back and stared at the ceiling, glad to have some time alone. My head was sore and my heart ached –

stretched by unanswered questions and what-ifs; broken by disappointment. I had swum in the deep end. I had risked everything. And for nothing. I still didn't know why people had to die and whether it could be stopped. And even though I had had the chance, I hadn't been able to save Granny Maggot.

I looked at my project book on the bedside table. I should have been eager to update it, but what was the point of trying to organise chaos? *I could write that down*, I thought; *it's a great saying*. But I didn't want to write anything or think about it any more. That's not like me at all, and I realised then that I was tired. Super tired. More tired than I'd ever been.

As I was about to turn out the lights, Dad came in. He sat on the edge of my bed and placed his hand on my chest.

'I'm sorry about your friend's granny,' he said, gently. I knew he'd be able to feel the quickening beat of my heart through my pyjama top. 'I had no choice.'

I sat up. 'So it was you?' I asked innocently as I could.

'It had to be me.'

'What do you mean?'

'It could have been different. If she hadn't gone when she was supposed to, it wouldn't have been so gentle. Trust me, Jim, it was her time.'

'But she wasn't *that* old! I've seen older people than her. I've seen people so old they look like tortoises! And Will's really upset,' I added, hoping that would explain why I was so passionate. It was part of the reason. The other part was that I just didn't understand, and I hate not understanding.

'Look, Jim. Mrs Maggot wasn't ancient, it's true. But she was ready.'

'How do you know?' I tried.

Dad shrugged. 'How do you know when a popcorn kernel is about to pop or when the first raindrop will fall? We know it's going to happen, but we don't know when.'

'But you *do* at The Dead End Office. *You* know when someone is going to die, don't you?'

'Yes, but sometimes it's only at the last moment – the eleventh hour. And we don't know *why*.'

Dad drew my head to his chest and stroked the back of my neck. I could tell by his voice that he was wondering whether to leave it there or give me more. *Give me more*, I begged him silently. *Give me more*.

'We have a special piece of apparatus, you know.' His voice was uncertain, but calm. 'This machine takes information – birthdays, gender, eye colour, blood type . . .' Dad hiccupped and trailed off. He shouldn't have mentioned blood.

'And?' I wrapped my arms around his middle and squeezed him for more.

'And it then gives us a death date.'

The Human Existence machine!

'That's really weird,' I sniffed.

'Yes it is,' Dad said, with a soft laugh. 'It was created long, long before my time – and it was created in many forms. Apparently, in the Stone Age, the Human Existence machine model was just a field with holes – each hole representing a day – and the Dead End Cave people would roll stones with people's names over the field. Plop! Whichever hole your stone went down, that was when your time was up!'

'But that's just . . . *random*! Is that true?' I pulled back, amazed.

'I have no idea. But I don't think it got used much anyway. They had a tendency to keep getting eaten by bears and sabre-toothed tigers. Grrrrr!'

Dad bear-hugged me until I shrieked and then he drew in a deep breath and let it out slowly.

'Seriously, Jim, you can spend a lifetime worrying over questions that can't be answered . . . It's sometimes better not to get out of your depth,' he whispered. 'Just enjoy what you have in front you, right here, today.' Dad stood up and fished something out of his back pocket. He unfolded a cap and placed it gently on my bedside table on top of my project book. It had a Happy Husk logo and a tyre mark across the front. There was no mistake – it was the one that fell in the gutter by Riverside Care Home. *He knew!*

'*Carpe diem*, Dad,' I gulped.

'Yes,' said Dad, looking surprised. Parents are always impressed by Latin. '*Carpe diem*,' he repeated, hugging me once more.

I lay awake for a long time after that, considering my talk with Dad and thinking back over the day of 'saving' Granny Maggot. It had only been a mere twenty-four hours, but it seemed like a lifetime. We had packed in adventure, fear, fun, family, food and Roberto's All-Night Funfair. Kevin was impossibly nice, Fiona laughed, Mrs Maggot made new friends and healed old wounds; Will was a total hero. And me? I might have failed – failed to save Granny Maggot – but I didn't regret a second of it.

The day of not saving Granny Maggot had taught me a few things, like family is worth fighting for and friends will piggyback you, not all people with Italian names are from Italy, and candyfloss is not good worn next to the skin. It also taught me that some contracts are 'today contracts' and can't be put off – and there's nothing you can do about them. But also, there is always Give and Take – a star is born, a star explodes; an old lady dies, a new baby arrives. At the end of the day Life and Death are just Random Acts of Randomness. It's all a universal experiment; so my advice is to stay up late when the funfair's in town, make the teacups go faster and laugh when your bus goes round corners.

Why? *Carpe diem*, that's why.

Acknowledgements

Thanks to friends and family for getting behind Jim Reaper. Thanks also to Jamie Littler for bringing the series to life, and to Alice Williams and Matilda Johnson. And huge hugs to my regular stable of readers – Jerome, Elise, Fleur, Emile, Ollie and Sammy. If I could, I'd take you all for a sugary sweets splurge at Streets the Newsagents!

*Look out for the next uproarious Jim Reaper
adventure about life, death and all the
hilarity in between ...*

JIM REAPER
The Glove of Death

When Mum asks Jim to rid their garden of
snails, he has an idea. Using the white glove
from Dad's study, Jim is going to give each
snail a swift and painless death. But can he
go through with it? When Mr Darcy the cat
gets involved, Jim loses the glove and
trouble breaks loose.

Can Jim avoid deadly disaster and
losing Dad his job?